This paperback edition p

Copyright © J.M.G.Smi

Paperback ISBN 979-8-3656-873-49

This book is a work of fiction. Names, characters, places and incidents are either a product of the author's imagination or are used fictitiously. Any resemblance to actual people, living or dead, events or locales, is entirely coincidental.

Printed by Amazon

The Unwelcome Resident

J.M.G.Smith

Chapter 1

An announcement came through over the loudspeaker.

"The train from Platform 3 is a direct train for St Louisham and will be leaving in 5 minutes."

The Great Western Train consisted only of two carriages and very few people, all bored and fed up and wondering when the docile train would ever leave. Opposite a train had just pulled into St Heliers, completely packed full of people, mostly businessmen and women. The doors flew open, and the travellers fell out almost on top of each other, in a bid to quickly disembark and be first to the gates. I watched the scene wearily resting my face on my hand and breathed hot air on the window. I hardly recognised my own reflection, the dark shadows under my eyes and the white hairs dotted in my thick dark hair. I still had two weeks left of sick leave to take, even though I was fully recovered after the accident, I just wanted to get back to work.

Suddenly with a lurch, the train slowly pulled out of the station, and gathered speed as the city was left behind. "Destination unknown," I murmured quietly to myself. Which strictly speaking wasn't true, I knew where I was heading, yet an unknown place awaited me. Fortunately, it was not a long trip, barely 20 minutes at the most. Soon I pulled alongside a small platform labelled St Louisham, I grabbed my suitcase and ambled slowly off the train. The first thing I noticed was the piercingly cold wind, it hit me unexpectantly. The station itself was based on top of a steep hill, with town houses scattered beside the roadside and down towards the sea. With no sign of a bus or taxi, I descended towards the town centre.

The houses were mostly painted white with pastel-coloured windows and doors, with dried up dead flowers in window boxes, and the first few leaves of autumn blustering about. Hardly anyone was about, the few people from the train had disappeared from view, presumably they lived in one of these houses. Trees creaked eerily in the breeze bending their branches low to the ground, a gate creaked back and forth on rusty hinges. Soon I alighted upon the town, the high street was slightly busier, as people hustled on with their shopping. A café sat on the corner of the main street, its windows all steamed up and gave off a warmth feeling of cosiness. I found myself sipping a hot coffee and asking the barista where one could get a taxi around here.

"It's Morecombe you want?" she asked.

"Yes. Do you know it?" I responded.

"Course I do. Nothing there though. Dead end place."

I almost rudely replied, 'Can't be deader than this backwater!' instead I politely asked, "So which direction do I go?"

"No chance. There are only three buses a day, you've missed the afternoon bus, left half hour ago. No taxi's round here either. Bob does the odd lift but he's off on his hols. Mostly we rely on each other for lifts."

There was a silence, I just looked at her wondering when she might say something useful and helpful instead of short irritating sentences. An elderly lady sitting behind me gave me a gentle prod in the back,

"Here, I can offer you a lift. I'm just visiting like, you know, the shops here are so much better. Take a look in my bags, only paid two quid on the cheese perfectly ripe like, and look at these gorgeous sausages, half price from the butchers!"

The woman was round and comfortably wrapped up in a thick warm rug like coat, she reminded me of my grandmother. Her face was gentle and kind, I felt myself warming to her and wasn't at all surprised when she offered me cake and tea, which I declined.

"My name is Ann." She said and held out a hand. "How do you do?"

"Tom." I replied, and formerly shook her podgy hand. "Do you have a car then nearby?"

"Gosh, in a hurry, are we? I don't drive like. My husband will be picking me up in about ten minutes. Oh! Look who is here and on time like."

I looked up towards the door as two more biddys entered and called out to Ann, all three of them talked at once about their successful trip. Various bags got unpacked, and items were compared and remarked upon, lots of 'ooh's' were heard. A tall man walked through the door, he had a large grin on his thin weathered face and looked extremely delighted to see such a happy bunch. My heart sank as he walked towards the crowd of women with his keys still in hand.

"This is Nigel," explained Ann, "He'll be driving us home."

"How do you do?" said Nigel. I gave a respectful nod of the head.

"We're giving this young man a lift Nigel."

"Course! No problem, plenty of room! Come ladies."

Nigel marched out through the door, followed by the ladies clucking like hens, I held the door open before straggling after them. A small little red Fiat Brava looking rather the worse for wear, was half perched on the pavement just around the corner.

"It might look dilapidated, but she still drives like a dream," Nigel reassuringly explained with a hearty laugh, throwing my suitcase and the bags in the boot. I on the other hand was not reassured at all, especially as the car sagged under the weight of the passengers. Hesitantly I clambered in, as Nigel pushed the rear door too, squeezing us all in. Morecombe was just around the other side of the bay, or so I thought, as Nigel turned the car around and headed up the steep hill back towards the station. The car groaned and struggled, with black fumes coming out the back and Nigel motivated the old girl to go on, I thought this must be the end. But it wasn't and it was a pleasant drive after that, along the main road by the cliff edge. We swerved off to the left along a small country lane through hedges, and then down a winding road, which opened up to a panorama.

"Nothing like home." One of Ann's friends declared.

Morecombe was beautiful, a little village by the sea edge in a cosy cove nestled between two large, towering cliffs. The sun shone down on the scenery giving off a false warm feeling, seagulls cried and sailed on the breeze, a few people on the stony beach gave the place a homely feel. The little car descended down the last part of the journey and parked up near the sea front.

"Here we go." Exclaimed Nigel, "Can't go further than this, it's the end of the road. A little piece of heaven it is out here."

We all climbed out of the vehicle and hovered by the wall.

"Thank you very much for the lift. Didn't realise it was such a difficult place to reach!" I said, grabbing my stuff.

"So, you know where you are and where you're going like?" Ann asked.

"The Red Lobster, I've booked for a few nights."

"Ooh, pricey like! They charge far too much for a room, but the breakfast is five stars! Now, follow the sea wall all the way round to the left. Can you see over there? A long white building all lit up. That's where you're going like."

"Well enjoy your stay in paradise, plenty of walks around here. Our post office can give you maps, advise, anything you need. It's also the grocery store. Well, it's been nice to meet you." Nigel reached out for a handshake. The ladies uttered pleasant goodbyes and gathered their bits and pieces before heading up a small alley squeezed between two rows of dainty houses.

*

A flamingo pink sunset lit up the sky as the last of the sun disappeared beyond the horizon of a golden sea. Gentle waves lapped gracefully on the shingle with a soft roar as it retreated back towards the ocean. Lamps and various lights from houses lit up as dusk set in, cats emerged from their hiding places as the promise of a moonlit night was on the cards.

The Red Lobster was set a little apart from the village and slightly up the cliffside, giving a full view of Morecombe when admiring it from the front door. To my surprise upon opening the door, I found the place full to the brim, every table was taken. Pushing past the locals, I found a spare bar stool on the corner and ordered a pint.

"What's going on?" I inquired, "Footy night?"

"Friday night, it's usually this busy on a Friday. You're new to these parts, are you visiting?" The barman replied, wiping a glass clean with a dirty cloth. "Wait. You're this Tommy Jones, I've got you down in my book. You're nothing like I thought you would be! Brian Fletcher, I own this place, it's been my pride and joy for going on thirty years now."

"Nice to meet you Brian," I murmured, watching the man flick through the pages of a tattered looking book. "So, what do you mean I'm not what you thought I was?"

Brian threw the book towards me with a pen, "Sign here. And I will need proof of I.D. and you're in. Nah, I thought you'd be an older bloke, a birdwatcher, or a retired mad scientist. You're much younger, so what are you?"

I tossed my card across the counter along with my badge, "Detective Inspector, here on business."

"Blimey, Detective Inspector, eh?" Brian gave a shrill whistle, handing back my badge. "Police business? So, what's going down dodgy?"

"You had a young girl who died from an accidental fall not far from here, her parents are not satisfied, so I'm looking into it. Nothing dodgy."

"Yeah, young kid, graduate from St Heliers University. About a month ago, weren't it?"

"Jenny Hops. Only twenty-three."

"Well good luck to you. Here's your key, room 8, up the stairs and last room on the right. Shared bathroom. I hope you have a good stay." Brian responded woodenly and turned his back to talk to some friends who had just walked in and joined the bar. I could feel the eyes and whispers all around me, so I took my cue and my key and headed to the room.

Chapter 2

Breakfast the next morning was excellent and definitely worth the five stars Ann had given it. The pub was completely empty and the streets outside were quiet, not a soul was about, human or animal. I finished my coffee and headed out into the cold crisp atmosphere, the wind had died down since yesterday, yet my eyes still stung and watered as the air hit my face. There were very few shops in Morecombe, the post office with its grocery store as Nigel had mentioned, a little café, a wool and crafts kind of shop which also had various giftware in the window. And a DIY store which had practically everything you could ever need, a mop set, lightbulbs, plant feed, and a large variety of screws, nails, nuts and bolts all set neatly in their right place in an organiser. I turned slightly up the hill towards a sign, dark blue with white writing, the police house door was also painted dark blue; I entered in.

"Morning. How can I help?" The man at the desk asked, twiddling a pen between his fingers and resting heavily on his arm, "Lost property? Car scratched? Cat in a tree?"

"Nothing like that," I responded, glancing behind the man at the other policemen who looked just as thoroughly bored, "It's about the girl who died here, Jenny Hops."

"Oh! Oh…I see. Right. Ok. Well Jacks is your man."

A tall, fluffy blond, skinny young man with immaculate uniform stood up and gave me a nod, "If you like to come with me?"

I followed suit along a small dimly lit corridor and into a private office at the back, the young man pulled out a chair for me, before heading to the break room to grab some refreshments for us.

"Constable Jonathan Jack, most folk here call me Jacks. So, you're wanting to know more about Jenny Hops, can I ask why?" He passed me a watery looking tea and soft biscuits that crumbled between my fingers.

"Detective Inspector Jones. Her parents asked me to look into the case, they're not satisfied it was accidental." I explained, taking a cautious sip.

"It was an open and closed case Jones. We didn't even need to take it up. Young girl walking about the cliffs at night, hardly surprising she slipped and fell."

"Her parents thought she was with someone at the time, she said she was going to Morecombe with a friend, possibly a boyfriend that she doesn't want her parents knowing."

"I'll bring you the file to read and you can ask me questions after, sorry I can't be of more help." Jacks stood up and left the room for a few minutes, before returning with a paper-thin file which he threw on the desk. "I'll leave you to it."

I opened the file which only consisted of one page:

Name: Jennifer Margaret Hops

Age: 23

Description: Slim, 5'6ft, brunette bob haircut, blue eyes, oval face, birthmark on the upper left arm near shoulder, tattoo of a butterfly on the right thigh.

Date Death Occurred: Wednesday 20th September 2022

Time Death Occurred: Approx. 10pm-2am

Type of Death: Accidental death from Misadventure.

Notes to add: None

On Wednesday the 20th of September, a call was received at 6.32am to a private home number of

Constable Jonathan Jack. The caller, an elderly man, name of Roger Hope, was walking his two dogs along the cliff. The dogs found the body, which was halfway down the cliff lying on some rocks. Police attended the scene at 6.50am, a cordon was put up in place, forensics attended the scene at 7.38am. Conclusion was an accidental death from falling from a high cliff. Death was from a severe concussion and further examination from St Heliers hospital led the conclusion to an internal bleed on the brain. Several scratches to the face and bruises to the back of the head coincided with the fall. A large bruise to the jaw however had occurred at least 12 hours before death.

A rucksack with a water bottle, a mobile phone, a credit card, house keys and a spare jumper were found tossed near a hedge. A torch was found on the ground near to where the deceased fell.

Her parents from St Heliers were duly interviewed and could give no further evidence or information as to why deceased was along the cliffs at that time of night. Residents were also interviewed, again no further evidence or information. A boyfriend, Sean Conway, a resident of Morecombe, was also questioned, further evidence showed that the deceased was living with him at time of death.

A signature from Constable Jack concluded the verdict.

I paused and reflected, pressing my fingertips against each other and tapped my thumbs. Accidental death was the final conclusion and the obvious answer, so why were the parents so insistent it wasn't? Suicide didn't look likely either, you don't take your belongings when you're about to jump off a cliff. I closed the file and headed back to the main entrance; Jacks walked over,

"Everything satisfactory, open and closed?"

"Looks like it. How did she fall?" I questioned, "Forwards or backwards? I'm assuming backwards?"

Constable Jack paused for a moment, "Yes. Backwards I think?"

"So, she fell backwards? But if she was walking casually along and fell, she would have fallen feet first and damaged her legs and more than likely fallen on her stomach or on her side. Bit unusual finding her on her back, isn't it? Unless she reached out to grab onto something to save herself, which is near impossible in the dark."

"Well…when you say it like that then yes, I suppose so. Haven't really thought about it before."

"Was she backing away from something? Or was she pushed backwards? Also, do you have the addresses for Roger Hope and Sean Conway?"

"I'll write it down, don't be surprised if they don't want to cough up anything. A lot of the people are friendly enough, but they don't like it when police swarm the place if you get my drift?"

"Perfectly, thanks Jacks, can I call on you again if I need you?" I asked, zipping up my thick coat.

"I'm here most days, if not, here's my card and home number but only call if it's important. If your washing has blown next door, or you've lost your house keys, don't call me!" Constable Jack chuckled, showing me the door.

I smiled and gave a small laugh "No chance of anything like that happening! Cheerio."

I glanced at my wristwatch, lunchtime. The café served prawn mayonnaise sandwiches with salty crisps with a crispy salad, washed down with bubbly lemonade. I decided after lunching my next protocol would be to seek out this Sean Conway, with him being the nearest on the list and the only house I knew where to find. A bright pastel blue house, which I happened to notice yesterday perched on the corner of Criers Hill; a large bronze number '1' hanged next to the white door which was impossible to miss. I rapped the door with my knuckles and a young surly lad cautiously popped his head out and rudely asked,

"Who are you and what do you want?"

"Detective Inspector Jones. I need to ask questions." I politely replied and delicately added, "About your girlfriend Jenny."

"God! So many questions! Did you know I had that young ass from the police station asking me questions every other day what I knew? He's sure I had something to do with it, he still gives me a hard stare each time we pass in the street."

"Right. It'll only take a minute. Her parents aren't convinced it was an accident you see."

"Wait… so you're accusing me as well! Aren't you? Her parents have decided I must be responsible and want me sent down for it?" Sean angrily responded, his face turning bright red and his eyes blazed, "Tell them they've got it all wrong!"

The young lad quickly took a step back and slammed the door fiercely in my face before I had time to answer, leaving me on the outside puzzling over what I had just said. I knew nothing more could be done at this address, so I glanced at the next place of call, The Maples, but no street name or number. I decided to ask at the post office, which was just around the corner, various crates of fruit stood outside it, attracting the village's winged insects. A young helpful lady behind the counter directed me on where to go,

"Follow the road in the direction of the pub, all the way round out of the village and along the farm track at the end. You can't miss it."

I courteously thanked her and continued on my way. The narrow road snaked around the picturesque seaside houses. It was clearly used by pedestrians as well as vehicles hence no pavements on the sides. A large gate barricaded the road with an access to

Morecombe Farm and Cottages only sign, an overgrown stile under ivy was the only way through. It was a steep ascension up the side of the hill, the main road had officially ended at the barrier, leaving a rough dirt track full of potholes and crumbly stones the rest of the way. Upon reaching the top, I was thoroughly out of breath and perspired rapidly under my coat which I swiftly removed. The landscape was in itself breath-taking, I could see for miles of flat slightly hilly fields of leftover stumps from harvested corn, and each field was contained in its own neat hedgerow box.

*

The Maples was the first cottage I happened upon, more of a large house than a cottage though, withered pink roses clambered up the front of the cottage and dangled off the porch. A front garden full of sedums, gladioli and golden rods were scattered amongst the spent summer blooms, with a small and pebbled pathway in between, leading to the front door positioned perfectly in the middle of the house. An elderly woman was peering out of the front window before moving out of sight and opening her door.

I called out to her, "Afternoon. Is Roger in?"

"Roger? Yes. He is in." She replied, beckoning me into the house and led me towards a comfortable looking sitting area. A large worn out weary looking red sofa was pushed against the wall, surrounded by a pair of similar looking armchairs. She waved an arm,

"Please, do sit. Roger will be in the greenhouse. His roses are his pride and joy. I'll fetch him for you."

A large cuckoo clock on the wall gave a loud chime and the bird popped out and back in again with swift force and a loud 'cuckoo,' which caused me to jump. Twice more it cuckooed. The door behind me opened, an elderly and slightly stooped man with a cane walked in.

"Afternoon," I said and introduced myself and held out a hand.

"Afternoon good sir." Roger replied, shaking my hand, "Come to the study man. Diana likes her afternoon programmes this time of day, and the knitting Nannas as I call them will be along by four."

"I shan't take too much of your time, just a few questions."

"Whiskey first my man, then questions. On the rocks?"

I nodded and followed him into a large yet very full room, bookshelves lined the whole side of the study. They were crammed to the brim with books and several smaller stacks of books lay piled on the floor. A small desk and two armchairs were perched in the only space left behind the door.

Roger handed me a finely cut whiskey glass, "Questions. We've had so many lately. Please sit."

I obediently sat down and glanced at Mr Hope, a slightly chubby man with a well weathered tanned face, and a finely trimmed white beard and moustache with a white mop of hair to complete the look. His eyes were bright blue and looked at me kindly and curiously. I opened the discussion,

"Jenny Hops."

"Ah yes. Poor lass. So young and just graduated I heard," said Roger pondering. "I found her on the cliff. Have you read the report?"

I nodded.

Roger continued, "Luna found her. Thought she was barking at a rabbit or a seagull. Not much otherwise I can tell you that you don't already know."

"Did you see her that night? Or a light from a torch?"

"Now that's a good question. I said to Jacks I think I saw a light about 11pm that night. But I was on the way to bed, and when you're tired and old and do-lally, these things can trick the mind."

"Was it just the one light, or was there another? Did you see anyone at all?"

"Yes, just the one light. And no, I saw no-one."

"Where did the accident happen can I ask?"

Roger arose steadily from his chair, grabbing his stick, "Come. Let me show you. Damn dogs will need a walk."

We donned our coats and left via the back door over the immaculate lawn dotted with apple trees towards a small white picket gate in between the picket fence. A pathway ran along the back of the house.

"That's the quickest way back to town," Roger explained, pointing his cane to the left of the path, back towards Morecombe. "It's all part of the coast path. The road is at least a mile further round, only cars use it."

"So do you think Jenny came up by the coast path?" I asked inquisitively.

"Oh definitely! You can access the coast path by the cottages which are all private property. The public's right of way is via Morecombe or Morecombe Farm. I can't imagine her walking two miles by the road in a bid to reach the cliffs, can you? What I would like to know is, why? Why was she up here that time of night?"

"It's a question I've asked myself many times."

We walked further up the path which was perched very close to the edge of the cliff and nothing to stop you from going over. After fifteen or so minutes Roger stopped and peered down,

"Here she was. Careful as you go. Don't want to report another body."

I slowly manoeuvred towards the edge and glanced down, sharp rocks spiked out of the beach and the waves lapped angrily against the stony pillars blocking their path. Seagulls floated below enjoying the sea breeze and the wind that held them up. A large rock projected out halfway down the cliff rock, a dark stain could still be seen and evidence of disturbance. As I headed slowly back to the path, I observed none of the grass or soil at the top had been uprooted or damaged. There was no sign of the young girl having tried to rescue herself. I turned round to Roger, and it was then that I noticed the house, half hidden behind overgrown trees, knee high grass and a broken picket fence. The house itself was severely damaged, the walls were crumbling and showing holes, yet the roof was still intact apart from a few gaps. Some of the windows were smashed, and the door had fallen off its hinges. Ivy and rambling white roses climbed up the side of the building, pulling down what was left of the guttering.

"What is that place?" I curiously asked.

"That is The Larches. We don't talk about that place. It's an evil place."

Chapter 3

Later that night I found myself brooding over my supper. That house, I couldn't get it off my mind. Why was it abandoned like that? And why did Roger say it's an evil place? And the girl, why was she up on the cliffs in the middle of the night? I needed to know, I wanted to know. I gave a deep sigh and cleared the rest of my plate. Tomorrow will be another day I told myself.

*

When I saw Jacks the next morning, he couldn't give any helpful advice on why the house was the way it was, nothing was in the police files. According to him, the place was always decrepit ever since he was a small boy and should be pulled down in his opinion.

Now I'm not one to usually give up, yet I reckoned with myself that I had hit a brick wall with the house, as for the girl, it was a clear and definite accidental death. I headed back to the pub, time to go home and give the parents the final verdict. I was packing the last of my clothes when there was a loud knock on my door.

"Packing up already, are you? You've still got some nights booked. Tired of this place? Can't blame you, you didn't look like a walker to me to be fair. Nothing left round here to investigate neither!" Brian gave a hearty laugh. "I was going to say room service. But I'll wait till you're gone. Do you need a pint before you head off? Bus isn't due for another hour and a half."

I cursed myself, I completely forgot about the infrequent buses, so I nodded, "I'll be down in ten."

Downstairs, families and couples were settled down, enjoying an early carvery lunch at a reasonable Sunday discount. Brian passed me a frothy looking pint of Carlsberg with a bowl of crisps.

"How did you enjoy Morecombe?" He asked, pulling pints for a group of men jostling each other at the bar.

I couldn't decide if Brian was being sarcastic or serious, I replied, "Your village is beautiful, and the residents are mostly friendly. Next time I visit it'll be when I'm taking a proper vacation."

"Did you find out about that girl?"

"Yes. Accidental."

"I could've told you that. Weren't too sure whether you were pointing at the locals to blame you see. I know these people, no-one around here could commit murder." Brian explained in a manner of matter-of-fact way. "Decent folk. Young lads do sometimes damage property and things go missing. The odd brawl breaks out, but we all draw a line at killings."

"Do you know exactly where she died?" I asked, wondering how much Brian knew. Judging by how continuously full the pub was, it was clearly the hub for local gossip.

"Course I do," Brian answered, coming over next to me and perched on a stool, and whispered, "Them cliffs. That house. Roger mentioned he was up that way with you yesterday afternoon."

I thought to myself and wondered how Roger managed to find the time to converse in the pub, I duly questioned, "What do you know about the house?"

"Ssh!" Brian exclaimed, and looked over his shoulder, "We don't talk about that house. Now all I can say is, is it's been derelict for years, even before I was born. My parents were teenagers at the time, friends with the daughter of that place."

My face must have shown confusion as Brian gave a large sigh and said, "Let's start from the top. The Larches don't know when it was built, but it was falling down when they lived there. Mr and Mrs Forest or Ferret or Fester. Whatever can't remember their name. Anyhow, they were killed, shot through the head at close range. Their girl Grace, newlywed left with her husband, I think they moved to the village. The husband was working up at the farm at the time and eventually took over, and then they lived there with their family. Grace has died now, can't speak for the husband."

It took a while for me to sort the facts in my head, "Do you know the name of Grace's husband? Or any of her children?"

"Nah can't remember the husband's name. I went to school though with Mike. Michael Barnes."

"Mike?"

"Grace's son, probably nearly sixty now same as me. He doesn't talk much about the family. You know he could be at the farm, worked for the Jackson's when we were kids."

"Did they catch who did it?" I inquired, eager to learn more.

"Nah." Brian answered, "This was the fifties though, police weren't thorough, and I don't believe the press released much info about the crime. Now if you want to find someone at the farm, best head round at supper time about six tonight. Them up there don't find their way to my pub, strictly isolated lot."

"This is all great, just what I needed to know. I should have asked you first!" I laughed and downed the last of my beverage.

"You'll be staying longer I take it?" Brian guffawed, "Given you another crime to solve. Not that you'll find anyone, I reckon the murderer is long dead and given a decent burial in the Churchyard."

"There's a Church?"

"St Lukes, at the top of Criers Hill. These days our dead are buried at St Louisham cemetery, peaceful spot in the middle of nowhere."

I thanked him again and drew out my notebook and wrote down all necessary information which could help this new investigation further.

*

Once more I found myself walking along Criers Hill, this time ignoring the large number one on the side of the blue house. All the curtains were shut tight, which meant either nobody was at home or that someone was keeping a low profile. The pathway was a steady climb and tranquillity hung in the air, until I approached the corner and a small crowd of people huddled around the Church gate. St Lukes was a small unique Church, more like a house with odd extensions either side of it, a steeple placed on top and then as an afterthought painted bright white. The service must have only just finished as a few more people filed out, two elderly women in flowery dresses with smart hats and little clutch bags, gave me a wave in recognition. I presumed that Ann must be somewhere nearby, these three ladies were inseparable! And on cue another female walked over to me, calling out as she did so.

"We meet again stranger. Tom, isn't it?"

"Hello Ann. Nice, to meet you again so soon." I responded courteously.

"We are in a village Tom. We're bound to bump into each other sooner or later like." Ann replied with a broad grin of her podgy face. "How's the holiday, all rested and enjoying ourselves I hope."

"Enjoying myself definitely. Resting…not so much."

"Well take the day off, like it's Sunday after all."

"I could, but I'm too inquisitive, I'm on a trail. Part of my job, to know things and find out things."

"You're not a reporter, I hope. The last one proper upset me and my girls like, rattled us all to the edge of tears." Ann looked exceedingly worried and fidgeted with her silk scarf.

I reassured her, "I'm not a reporter, I'm a detective."

"Oh!" Gasped Ann, "That's even worse!"

I was bewildered and stuttered, "I'm sorry to alarm you, I didn't realise you weren't fond of the police."

"It's not the police like. It's what you discover, the secrets, the people you love being suspects, the interrogation. The mess you police officers leave behind like," she whimpered, crying softly into a tissue. A gentle whistle could be heard on the gravel and getting louder as someone approached them, it was the vicar.

"Nigel the vicar! I didn't recognise you in your costume!" I cried out astonished, "To think you gave me a lift and I had no idea! I'm sorry about Ann I didn't mean to upset her."

Nigel laughed, patted my back and then placed a loving arm around Ann and addressed her, "Now then. What's the fuss? What's going on my love?"

"Tom is a detective, Nigel. You know how I feel about policemen." Ann quietly murmured.

"Don't worry Tom, it's not you. Come over for lunch, we can talk this over then. I'm famished," said Nigel. And then he said to Ann, "I'm sure he's not here to investigate us and one policeman can't do any harm."

Ann silently nodded and we proceeded down a small, pleasant path which ran through the Church, a tall gate positioned delicately between a low stone wall opened up into a large garden. Apple trees were carefully planted in a row either side of the garden, their leaves bare and most of their leftover fruit was scattered and rotting on the immaculate green lawn. Various viburnums were dotted along the outer edge and a mixture of autumn bedding were squashed yet flowering in the space underneath. There was no path to the back door, so we ambled where we pleased, it was a slightly raised garden which gave a good view through the trees of the Church and the sea behind. I could visualise myself in a place like this, but obviously I was in the wrong job, and I needed a closer connection with God first. Nigel unlocked the door. I entered and removed my shoes before following through to the sitting room. Ann had already opened the French doors to their fullest extent, and an autumn breeze that was surprisingly warm for that time of year blew through. I relaxed in a rocking chair and enjoyed the elderflower cordial that the vicar had given me. There was a moment where we just looked at each other, unsure what to say in the fear of upsetting one another.

Nigel broke the silence first, "It's lovely to have you here Tom. It's very rare to have people visit our village, people usually just stop on their way through. Ann stood up and left to check on the lunch, leaving us men to talk.

It was a pleasant lunchtime meal, and we didn't elaborate any further on the situation of my profession. Instead, we told stories of our lives, our failures and our successes in our work, funny stories came about of various parishioners hilarious and unfortunate mishaps. It was almost three o'clock when Nigel and Ann declared they had other appointments to keep. I wrapped myself up and laced up my shoes hurriedly in a bid to no longer detain them more than necessary. Nigel left first, he had a time schedule for visiting the local residents and couldn't afford being late. Ann was arranging her woolly hat in the mirror in the hallway when she suddenly asked,

"Do you want to come with me? I'm seeing the girls. We usually meet up Sunday afternoons for tea like. Bit of gossip. Nigel doesn't care for that thing. Gossip is evil in his eyes."

I was unsure how to respond, I had it in my head that Ann was nervous of me and wanted to keep distant. I hesitantly said, "Sure, I mean…if you're ok with it?"

Ann laughed till her face grew red, "Bless you Tom. I apologise for earlier. It was rude of me like. Don't know what came over me. You've met Cathy and her house is just down the road near the seafront."

I graciously accepted her apology and together we headed back down Criers Hill to the sea and turned left away from the main street then left again up the small siding which I had noticed on my arrival. I was surprised when Ann took me around the back of a pale primrose yellow coloured house and through a side gate. A small stony staircase jutted out of the back of the house leading to a white door, a string of white lights wove their way up the railings and finished at an impressive pair of white lamps sitting in pots of flowers by the entrance. Ann didn't ring the doorbell, she opened the door and cried out cooee, and we let ourselves in and through to the main living area. It was a cosy little maisonette, the kitchen and bathroom were tiny, yet the living room and bedroom were plentiful in size. I admired the view from the window, mostly only the village could be seen, but by craning my neck I could make out the blue sea. Cathy sat by the window in her recliner chair, crocheting what she said was mittens for the newly born babies at St Heliers Hospital. Another call came through and the party was complete, the woman who entered introduced herself as Sylvia, and she had brought plenty of cake. I was still feeling very full from a smashing lunch, but I politely accepted a slice and a cup of tea. It didn't take long for the gossip to commence.

"Tom. How's your holiday? Pleasant, I hope?" Cathy asked whilst still looking at her handicraft.

"Very," I mumbled with a mouthful and swallowed, "Very peaceful in these parts."

"I'm surprised you managed to get here at all," retorted Sylvia, stirring her dainty cup, "You should have looked at the bus timetable or arranged a lift. Do you drive?"

"I do drive, but I preferred this time to travel by train."

"Unusual for a policeman to go without a car. I couldn't see how it could be done like, not in these parts. I suppose there is always cycling, they used to in the olden days." Ann declared, helping herself to another Foxes biscuit. The other ladies agreed in unison.

I decided to make a clean abreast of things, "I had an accident at work, a late-night raid about a month ago, my leg got damaged, so I've been told to rest before taking up driving again."

The ladies perked up their ears and their eyes widened, they restrained themselves to appear calm, whilst secretly on edge to know more.

"Do tell!" Cathy exclaimed excitedly, dropping her ball of wool on the floor.

"Nothing to tell," I said modestly leaning back, the eager faces weren't satisfied, so I continued, "We had information of illegal goings on in a warehouse. We took them unawares and arrested them on the spot. Of course, there were a few men who wouldn't go down without a fight. Next thing I know, I've got a flesh wound to my arm from a bullet and a stab wound in my leg. Woke up in hospital the next morning."

"You're so brave." Sylvia cooed, fluttering her eyelashes like a bashful schoolgirl.

I turned a bright red and tried not to look too pleased with myself.

"Such an exciting life." Sighed Cathy, returning to her crochet project, "We've not had anything like that happen around here in a long time."

"There was a girl who died recently, fell off a cliff. That was fairly exciting. Not the death I mean, but having forensics, police officers and reporters swarming the place." Sylvia piped up, filling up the teacups again, "And that boy before, he went down the same way."

"Was that in the same place?" Cathy asked.

"Exactly the same place."

"Urgh, how awful. Tom, what do you know about that place?"

I reckoned I knew what we were now discussing, the unmentionable, "That house, The Larches."

"That's right. Bad things happen to those who go near the place." Cathy responded eerily lowering her tone of voice. "So many gruesome and ghastly deaths."

"Cathy is exaggerating," Sylvia laughed cheerily, "It's just a house that's a little worse for wear."

"It's more than a house. Did you know Tom that a couple were shot there? Lying in their bed enjoying a lie in. The murderer just walked in, stared them in the face and kaboom, snuffed them just like that."

"Maybe he just wanted to put them out of their miseries. I mean, they were pretty near death like." Said Ann.

"Well, you don't blast someone's face off with a shotgun. You do it kindly, too many sleeping tablets in their tea or similar for instance. No, this was cold blooded murder. You can still see the stains left behind. Everything in the house has been left exactly the way it was, nothing taken. Their daughter moved out to the village, and I think afterwards she married."

"I was only a child when it happened," whispered Sylvia, "Police were everywhere. Turning out our homes, interrogating each of us in turn. They never did find the shotgun. That was the problem, so naturally whoever had a shotgun in their possession was treated like a murder suspect."

"And did they have any suspicion on who did it?" I curiously asked.

"My father. The police were convinced he did it." Ann mumbled, her eyes welling with tears, "He had a shotgun recently fired, hunting rabbits he said. He had no witnesses either and he recently had an argument with Grace, the young girl of the murdered couple. Turns out they were seeing each other like, she had no idea he was married or had kids. Mum was convinced he did it too. So, when the police released him because the evidence wouldn't hold, mum refused to let him home like. Don't know what happened to him. I was so young, so instinctually I blame the police, always have done. Like, they broke up my family, we were a really happy family, never been the same since that day."

Ann fled the room, unable to control her tears, Sylvia left to console her. Cathy cleared her throat, "Strictly speaking they weren't a happy family. Now I'm only a few years older than Ann, but I knew more than she did. And her dad…he was an alcoholic and a thug. No one dared cross him, hell for those who did."

"Do you think he was responsible?" I asked, my mind racing at the thought of a potential murder suspect.

"Oh definitely! Definitely."

Chapter 4

We sat in silence after that, pausing and reflecting on matters of the past, Ann and Sylvia were still next door, conversing silently over a boiling kettle.

"What was the name of Ann's father?" I asked, peering solemnly out of the window as rain drops began to fall.

"Colin Marsh. He is dead now. You'll find him in St Lukes graveyard. Died the way he lived his life, as a drunk. He never left Morecombe. I believe he moved in with a girlfriend he was seeing on the side. Adulterer that man, so many innocent girls played for fools." Said Cathy, cutting the strand of yellow wool from her finished project. "Two little mittens. And more babies to come this winter, I imagine."

"Did I hear right when Sylvia mentioned another person dying in the same place as Jenny?"

"Did she? Oh yes, a young boy. Gosh, that was years ago! You need to ask Ann. I believe it was her Nigel who found her."

Ann was still in the kitchen, I felt that I had upset her enough for one day, she was such a sensitive soul. I could easily ask her or Nigel another day, my mind was still intrigued with the double homicide, an unsolved mystery waiting to reveal itself.

I decided to change the subject and asked Cathy more about herself, turned out she was a midwife from early age right up to retirement. She had won a few certificates and awards over the years for her work successes and deliverance of several babies into the world. I wasn't in the slightest bit interested, and struggled to stay awake, my stomach was so full, and the room was so warm and comfortable. Fortunately, Ann and Sylvia had returned and were collecting their things and packing the remaining cakes into their cake boxes.

"We'll be off now. It is rather late like, Nigel will be wondering," said Ann, "Thank you for a pleasant evening."

"Yes, thank you Cathy. Next week Ann's place." Sylvia reminded, "I have so many Christmas ideas to discuss, I thought maybe this year we could add more tinsel to the Church and lights for the trees outside. We used so much holly last year it was so wasteful."

"If you remember Sylvia, the chap whose holly it was, was removing it completely from his garden. He didn't want it anymore, kept scratching him every time he left the house, you could hear him swearing from miles around!" retorted Cathy, standing up to embrace her friend's goodbye.

"Till then, see you soon. Bye!"

"Bye!"

I also took my leave and followed after Ann and her friend. I found the tables had turned between me and Ann, I was the one apologising profusely, whilst Ann graciously accepted. She left and went on her way back towards the Vicarage, whilst I ambled back towards The Red Lobster.

*

Another morning dawned in Morecombe, a cloudier and damper day with drizzle sweeping through and the raindrops getting heavier and louder by the minute. A good morning to scribble down some notes I thought to myself and enjoy a hearty meal in a very warm breakfast room.

Notes:

1. *Jenny Hops, died from cliff 20th of Sep. Possible suspect, Sean Conway.*
2. *Young boy died same way years ago. Need to ask Ann or Nigel for facts.*
3. *House 'The Larches' derelict for years, couple who owned it Mr and Mrs F. Shot in the face or head.*
4. *Grace, daughter of Mr and Mrs F. Dead now. Husband? Her son Michael Barnes lives at the farm.*
5. *Ann's father Colin Marsh deceased - arrested and released in connection with Mr and Mrs F's death.*

Satisfied I closed my notebook. The rain had eased off now and the sun was penetrating though the clouds, the village sparkled and glistened in the light. I decided a walk would do me good, and now I was finally by myself I could do what I wanted to do for a long time. Investigate. I took a spare jumper, socks, a torch, water, and some food just in case. The coast path was easier to find, now I knew where the entrance was, an unmarked path two doors down from the pub. Several steps zigzagged and climbed up to the top of the cliff, two hundred or so in total, I was relieved when the path levelled out. After passing the first house which I recognised as Roger and Diana's I soon passed the second and then there it was, the third house. The one I was looking for.

The Larches, still sitting precariously close to the edge of the cliff, with its tall grass that swished and blew wildly in the breeze. For a moment I paused. I took a deep breath and crept through the foliage, avoiding the nettles and brambles that leaned towards me. I peered through the back door, it was dark and musty inside, and eerily silent, no noise could be heard. Cautiously I took a step over the threshold, flickering on my torch as I did so. It was exactly as Cathy said, untouched, nothing moved, nothing seemed to be taken, thick dust and cobwebs lay everywhere. Plant debris and animal waste covered the floor, a dead bird which was mostly decomposed lay on the kitchen counter. I gave the sofa a little poke, several insects fled out of the ripped fabric and a small whiskered nose popped out. I shuddered. Mice weren't my favourite of creatures. A resounding crash echoed through the house, what sounded like furniture, or something had fallen upstairs. A floorboard creaked, feet padded across the floor and then the uncanny silence.

I stopped and listened. Panic was trying to take over me, but I quickly reassured myself it was only animals. I cleared my throat and silently headed to the bottom of the stairs and shone my torch up. A couple of portraits stared down at me, their eyes glowering in the light. I climbed the steps one at a time, my heartrate accelerating with each step I took. Finally, I reached the top. The small holes in the roof acted as skylights, and a quick sweep of the place revealed nothing and no-one. I deducted I was right, it was probably an animal, the house seemed full of them and plenty of entrances to let them in. The room nearest to me was full of past memorabilia of a young girl growing up, it lined the bookshelves and the vanity desk which had a mirror attached. The drawers and wardrobe were empty, and the bed was stripped bare, clearly a few things had been taken. I entered the room next door, this was obviously the master bedroom, judging by the size and a large double bed lying plonk in the middle of the room. A few rotting books lay on the remaining shelves, and three photographs sat on the windowsill, a wedding photo, a young girl, and a family picture. It was only when I swung my torch back round, that I noticed the blood stained and splattered wall, the bed must have been moved forward by forensics. Feeling rather sick to the stomach, I made my exit, I had seen enough.

As I was descending back downstairs on the creaky steps, another loud bang could be heard, right behind me this time. I froze. Trying not to panic. I swung the torch round rapidly, hoping to see something to calm my fears. There was no-one. There was nothing. I couldn't for the life of me figure out where or what that noise was. The place was creeping me out, so I quickly hurried back towards the back door and suddenly I felt something crackle under my feet. A golden bracelet with charms, I noticed that the chain link was broken. I wondered why I didn't see it when I walked in. It wasn't covered in dust or cobwebs, it looked more recent than that. I didn't want to jump to conclusions because it could be anyone's, yet something told me it was Jenny's. I stood back up to leave, glancing once more towards the kitchen, the crow on the counter was gone.

*

"Cat got your tongue?"

I dazingly raised my head and blinked, "What?"

Brian chuckled and sprayed more Dettol in my direction, "What's with the silent talk? Looks like you've seen a ghost mate! I said, bar is closed. Don't reopen till 4pm, this dirty palace needs a good scrub."

"Sorry Brian. Had a strange morning. Don't know what to think."

"Christ! This man needs a beer, have one on me! You need it," exclaimed Brian. He clearly believed in the home comforts of drink. He poured me a half pint and then poured himself one. "So, where we at?"

"With what?" I asked, still feeling rather confused.

"You know. That house. Pete saw you headed up the coast path, I said to myself there can only be one reason for someone to head that way. And he's got no dog so it's not that!"

"Oh right. I went in that house." I paused. I could no longer think of what to say. "Is it full of animals would you say. Or something more unearthly?"

"There are animals there all right. Unearthly, nah."

"That's what I thought."

"Then what's with the long face? It's just a house, isn't it? A house with a long story though, I give you that!" Brian swigged down the last of his ale.

"Why didn't Grace clear out the house, or arrange someone to do it for her?"

"Don't know mate. And we will never know neither. Right, I need to crack on. Darts night, starts at 8pm if you're interested."

I took the hint, and gathered myself before heading to the village, I fancied a trip to St Louisham. Glancing at my watch, I reckoned I had about six minutes to reach the post office in time for the 12:16. The rest of the day passed comfortably, shops and cafés, throwing round pebbles into the sea, a breezy walk and hot donuts along the pier. By the time the afternoon bus arrived I felt completely restored and ready to continue on the mission to uncover the truth.

*

It was nearly 6pm when I reached the farm, it was further round by road than I realised and took me an hour to reach. Mooing cried out from the barns, the fence rattling as the herd pushed their way to the front, along with the sound of a broom vigorously sweeping the hard floor. A large green tractor rumbled in the distance, weaving its way up and down the field. As I walked up to the farmhouse, a large black Labrador barked ferociously, barring his teeth at me. I could sense a standoff, so I glared at the dog, whilst debating whether to walk up to the door or not.

"ELVIS! QUIET!" a voice bellowed from the barn, the boy looked at me and said, "He's harmless. Looking for someone?"

"Michael Barnes? I was told he could be here?"

"Bottom field. Some of the stupid ewes are expecting, Mike's down there sorting one out." Explained the boy, returning to his sweeping.

"Right." I answered. I assumed the dirt track down towards where I saw the tractor was the right direction to go. My shoes got muddier as the track started to sink, I reached the end of the field and couldn't see anything or anybody. Where was the bottom field? A tanned man, past his prime in age yet still young, dressed in proper country attire and wellington boots called out,

"You lost?"

"Very, where's the bottom field?"

The man laughed and I immediately felt aggravated, there wasn't anything funny about sinking into mud and being lost in a field, the chap answered casually, "Go back from where you came. Then take a right and follow the track."

"Thank you." I pulled my feet out of the sticky mud and squelched my way back. This was not a good ending to the day. I found the path easily enough though, a small, cobbled track between old fashioned stone walls. Eventually it ended in a grassy paddock, several sheep and a few lambs roamed in front of a picturesque sunset. What a beautiful place to work, if only I could bring myself to face the elements. I couldn't see anyone, so once again I felt defeated, this was truly a very unfriendly environment! And once again I headed back to the farm, the young boy had gone, probably finished for the day. The cows had calmed down now and were happily grazing on some hay, their last meal for the night. Passing the farmhouse, I noticed the dog had now gone and a few lights were turned on in the farmhouse. That must mean someone is finally home, I rang the doorbell. Barking and shouting was heard, and the door swung open, and there he was, just standing there!

"And you're back again! I'm Michael Barnes. Pleasant to meet you," he held out a hand, which I rudely ignored, Michael withdrew his hand and responded with, "No? Ok. Did you find what you needed in the bottom field?"

I was already annoyed, but this really sent me over the edge! I angrily spluttered, "You! How dare you and why did you send me to the bottom field? You knew I was looking for you!"

The man calmly replied, "Firstly you asked me for directions to the field. Secondly, I didn't know you were looking for me, how could I know?"

"Well, what do you think I was doing? Wandering all over your bloody farm for the fun of it? You could have asked, oh who are you looking for?"

"Look. It's been a long day. Come in and have a drink," Michael retreated indoors, grabbing Elvis by the collar and tugging him towards the conservatory at the back. "Well come in. Shut the cold out."

Feeling like I had no choice I entered.

"Can you take your shoes off? They're very muddy." He called from the kitchen. "Will stella be ok?"

I took a deep breath in, to control my temper, before unlacing my boots and walking through the hall. It was certainly a very rustic country house, deer heads lined the wall up the stairs, a pair of shotguns were hanging above the kitchen doorway. A few display cabinets in the living room contained stuffed animals 'all captured on my farm' Michael had proudly added. A vintage table with stuffed flowers in a vase and high back wooden dining chairs sat between them and the conservatory. A sorry looking Elvis breathed heavily on the glass and gently pawed the door, hoping I would react and let him in. Michael bent down to restock the fire and closed the oven door firmly, before settling into a comfy armchair similar to mine.

"Cheers!" he said and took a long sip. "Aah, nothing better to release the tension."

I nodded, no longer sure how to approach this arrogant man.

Michael wasn't deterred, "You wanted me. So, let's jump straight to it. What do you want from me?"

I decided it was best to get straight to it, sooner I got what I wanted, sooner I could leave. I explained the basic facts which led me to this point, "Am I right in thinking your mother was Grace Barnes?"

"You got that right. There's a picture of her on top of the fireplace."

I stood up and recognised the girl from the picture at The Larches. She was in her wedding dress, still stunning as ever with her long brown hair and radiant smile. The man next to her wasn't smiling though, he looked solemn and serious in his dark suit.

"Is that your father?" I asked, placing the picture carefully back on the mantlepiece.

"Yes. Nathan. In a retirement home in St Louisham. I took over from him you see."

"Do you have any other siblings?"

"Cor. Nosey, aren't we? Tell you what. Why don't we arrange a proper day? Yeah. Then I can give you all the details, everything you want to know." Michael replied, folding his arms in a hostile manner, leaning back in his chair. "I think I've said enough. Now it's getting late. Do you mind seeing yourself out? Seeing as I didn't properly invite you over."

I stood up and manoeuvred to the front door, "One more question. Have you been to The Larches?"

"NO! And I never will! That place is cursed. No more questions!"

I sighed, pulled my shoes back on, grabbed my coat and left. It was extremely dark now. I swore to myself when I realised, I had forgotten my torch. My phone torch was so feeble I could only just see my feet, I realised it would have to do if I wanted to get back to The Red Lobster. Halfway down the road my eyes were blinded by an oncoming car, I held my hand in front of my face and stepped to one side, narrowly missing a large pothole. The vehicle slowed down and a woman got out,

"Hello there! What's possessed you to walk down a road late at night in the dark? Are you mad? You could walk off the cliff if you're not careful."

Strictly speaking that wasn't true, the cottages and their large gardens protected me from the cliff edge, and it wasn't possible to stray off the gravelled road by accident. I feebly replied, "I forgot my torch."

"Get in, I'll give you a lift to Morecombe. That is where you're going?"

I nodded and climbed into the Land Rover, "Thank you, it is extremely late."

"Nonsense. I'm Linda, I live next door to the Hopes. You met Roger and Di?"

She swiftly turned the car around using one of the driveways of the cottages. Before I could reply, Linda carried on talking.

"They have lived there for donkey years, we only moved in ten years ago ourselves. I own the café, you seen it I presume. My husband Arthur is a cars salesman, not here of course, over in St Louisham. That's where all the exciting stuff happens. I wanted to live there but Arthur likes the rural side of life, we found The Pines and we both fell in love with it. So, we moved here. What brings you to Morecombe? Settling down too, or just a fleeting visit?"

"Well." I began, and tried to keep it simple, "At the moment I'm looking into the old house, The Larches. Just been to visit Michael actually."

"Oh him. Rude man and so arrogant. If I was his mother I would set him straight, that attitude wouldn't wash with me. You wonder why his wife left him. Took off one night and with both kids, I believe they went to live with her mother. Runs in the family, his dad was just as bad if not worse! You never met the dad Nathan, have you? No, I thought not. He left only recently to a care home, best thing for him really, showing signs of dementia. His temper was horrific, apparently Grace would regularly come to Church with the young ones, a new bruise added to her persons. He wasn't always like that though. You need to talk to Roger. Apparently, he was quite the charming gentleman when Grace first met him." Linda paused to change gears as the road sloped downhill.

Which gave me time to ask, "So Grace left Nathan?"

"Gosh no. Did I say that? Grace stuck by Nathan, they had four children, so it can't have been all that bad. She's sadly died now so have two of her children. Michael is at the farm. Lydia is in the village. Me and Lydia work together, did you know? I took over from her, but she still works at the café and does the main bulk of the work. It was Roger who got in touch with her and got me the job in the first place. Did you know Roger worked for Nathan? Nathan let them carry on living at The Maples, which was really good of him, but now his son Michael wants them evicted, us too. He's been offered a good deal to build a caravan park up here, can you imagine it? A holiday park! Outrageous! You should come to the council meeting and help vote against it. Thursday night, I'll expect you there! Right, here's the gate. It's well-lit from here on, don't mind walking the rest, do you? I'll be glad to get off home, just as soon as the car is turned around. It's been really pleasant to meet you."

"You too. I appreciate the lift." I thanked, clambering out of the car and slamming the door.

Linda wound down the window and called out, "Anytime! Bye!"

Her car unsteadily turned around and skidded slightly before heading back up the hill, her red taillights soon disappeared from view. I turned on my heel and headed towards the pub.

*

"Where have you been? Thought you'd be back just before 7?"

Linda replied, "Giving a young man a lift, he was wandering around here, found him on the road would you believe."

"What was he doing up here?" Arthur quickly interrupted, knowing his wife's rambling habit.

"Visiting that young idiot at the farm. He's called Tom apparently. Frequenting the house next door, God knows why. Nothing to see at all. A very quiet boy, hardly said a word at all in the car!"

Chapter 5
1958

A sunny March Day shone on Morecombe. The weather was unusually warm for that time of year with a feel of spring in the air. Daffodils, crocuses, tulips and cherry blossom were on the verge of blooming, birds sang in the trees once more and the scenery was looking greener by the day.

A slim looking lady in her late fifties laid a basket of washing down, placed a few dolly pegs in her mouth, and proceeded to hang up the wet clothes. Clearly there was something not quite right with her health, every so often she stopped and placed two hands on her back and rubbed. After a while, another girl, much younger in age, came outside and helped the woman to finish off the laundry. Her long brown hair loosely plaited, fell apart and blew in the wind and curled around her round chin. With strong arms, she helped her mother inside again and settled her down on the sofa, before fetching a cup of tea.

"You need me." The girl said, "I can't leave you now, not whilst you're still recovering."

"You worry too much Grace," her mother answered, "I'm fine. Doctor said in a few more weeks I'll be fit as ever before."

Grace shrugged off what her mother said, she was going to stay put and that was that. After making tea, she set about cleaning the house and tidying up, putting the place to rights as they would say. Tapping on the floorboards from a wooden cane sounded upstairs and called for her attention. She sighed and placed a pot of tea with sandwiches on a tray, and carefully climbed upstairs.

"Afternoon Papa."

The man in the bed grunted and struggled to pull himself upright, "Get them curtains girl, feels like the gloom and doom of death in here."

Grace obediently did as she was asked, helped her father up, and offered him some tea, "Doctor's orders. Green tea, twice a day. No caffeine."

"Take it away! Stuffs terrible! Get some coffee will you. If I'm going to die, I want to die drinking and eating what I love most. And these sandwiches are the worst! Where's that cake your mother made? Am I deprived of that as well?"

"Doctor said…"

"Doctor this! Doctor that! Get me some cake! If you don't, I'll make your mother do it. At least she has respect and does as she's told. You're getting horribly rebellious! Get out!"

Obediently Grace headed back downstairs, her mother had fallen asleep on the sofa; she covered her with a blanket and kissed her forehead. Grace grabbed a red scarf and wound it round her own head, grabbed a basket and left for the village. The village stores were still open, and their wares were spilling out into the main road. Her first place of call was the post office to drop of some letters and buy a local paper and some baccy for her dad. A few doors down the local grocers were selling apples, unfortunately it was too soon for soft fruit. There were some very bruised looking oranges though, she had to decide whether to take it or leave it. Grace decided to leave it and brought twice as many apples to make up. Next door she bought half a dozen of freshly prepared sausages and some bacon and eggs for breakfast. As she was coming out of the butchers she bumped into her friend Lou,

"Hi Lou!"

"Hi Gracie, doing shopping for your folks?" Lou replied, eyeing the basket.

"As usual," Grace replied and covered the meats with a thin handkerchief, "Mum is getting worse, dad is the same."

"I like your mother, I'm sorry Gracie. I'll come over to help when I can. You know Ian can make amazing cakes, I'll get him to make one and I'll bring it over."

"Thanks Lou, be sure to sneak it in round the back though. Dad is on a diet!" Grace giggled.

"Sure! Hey, you free tonight? Me and Ian are going out to The Red Lobster. You should come. Ooh, bring that mystery guy you're seeing. Then it can be doubles!" Lou begged, pressing her hands together and looking like someone in prayer pleading for a miracle.

Grace sighed and shook her head slowly, "No. I, I can't. I'm sorry."

"Gracie. You cannot spend the rest of your prime and youth looking after your folk twenty-four seven. Their time is done, they've enjoyed their youth. It's your time now, and it's only for a few hours, and they'll be asleep anyway. 8pm sharp and bring that man of yours."

Grace laughed for she knew she was beaten, and it would give her a chance to try on her new dress her aunty gave her for Christmas. The girls hugged and promised to see each other later and retreated in opposite directions. Grace slowly ambled home, stopping to talk to more people and passed the rest of her afternoon in enjoyment.

When she reached the house, she was surprised to find the front door carelessly left wide open. She was sure she had closed and locked it, knowing how paranoid her mother was with strangers coming in. Cautiously she popped her head through and called out to her mother. But it wasn't her mother who replied, it was a different voice that came from the kitchen,

"Hello Grace thought I'd pop by. Finished early at the farm today, see. And I was wondering if you want to go out with me to St Louisham? There's a new restaurant opening tonight. Jeff offered me a ride. He's heading that way later."

Nathan Barnes, a rude young man who had a knack for turning up uninvited and expecting everyone to be thrilled and say yes to his silly proposals. Clearly, he had picked the lock again and let himself in, which was by law called trespassing. Nathan didn't care for laws for he did as he pleased and didn't worry about consequences or getting in trouble with the local police. He had recently been locked up for a night for a drunken brawl outside the local pub, whilst the other man involved was sent to St Heliers Hospital with a broken jaw. And yet girls were besotted with him and would blush and come over all shy when he asked them out for a date.

Grace made her way to the kitchen, casually ignoring him sitting on the counter and immediately threw the sausages and bacon into the fridge. Placed the apples in a sieve to be washed and the loaf of bread into the bread tin, she then turned around and said,

"Thank you, Nathan. I can't. I'm going out later with Lou."

Nathan rudely responded, "You? You never go out! You just stay here all the time playing mother to your own parents. I'll pick you up at 8pm. See you later Grace."

And with that he walked out of the house and unnecessarily slammed the door behind him, causing the house to shake a little.

Her mother woke up startled, "Who's that?"

"It's only Nathan Mama."

"What did he want?"

"Nothing."

The thumping noise from upstairs came again, Grace's father was once more calling for her undivided attention.

"Yes Papa?" Grace calmly asked once she reached his bedside.

"That man. I've told you before. He's not allowed in this house! And as for slamming doors! The roof is sagging my girl, the brickwork is collapsing all around us! Now, you tell him to stay away, or I'll call the police."

"Yes Papa."

Grace ran back downstairs and called out to her mother, "I'm going out. I'll be back later to cook supper."

With that she swiftly departed and at a gentle run she made her way up to Morecombe Farm. Partridges weaving nests in the long grass took wing in fright, birds in the hedgerow sang and fluttered about excitedly. A farm worker on his little tractor in the distance gave a cheery wave as he recognised her going about her way. Grace eventually arrived at the farm and rapped on the farmhouse door. A gentle looking woman with long blond hair tightly plaited, and a skinny body in tight breeches opened it,

"Hello Grace. Do you need my telephone again?"

Grace blushed, knowing that this must be becoming a habit, "Hello Susan. Yes please."

"I'll leave you to it. Horses need tending too." Susan opened the door further to let the young girl in, before setting off down the track next to the barns.

Grace deftly picked up the phone and called a local number knowing that the respondent should be home by now. After a few rings there was an answer on the receiving end,

"Hello?"

"Colin. It's me. Grace."

"Hello sweetheart. How are you? Not keeping too busy I hope?" Colin replied in his soft silky voice.

"Not too much. Are you free tonight? I'm meeting Lou and her boyfriend at The Red Lobster. She was hoping that me and you could make doubles."

"Doubles, eh? Sure. Why not. It will be a hoot! Can't stay too long though I've got work in the morning."

"I'll meet you there." Grace responded and hanged up the phone. A slight rustling noise came from the hallway. When she stood up to look there was no-one there, whoever it was must have left sharply. The only sound she could hear was the front gate which was swinging on its hinges.

*

Grace stood nervously on the corner, fidgeting with her blue shawl and glanced at her watch, "ten minutes late," she muttered to herself. She decided to wait another five minutes and call it a night, the locals in the pub sounded rowdy and the idea of walking in by herself was very off putting. Grace assumed Lou and Ian were in there already, but she couldn't see them from the little window by the main entrance. Finally, she glimpsed her boyfriend jogging slowly towards her and slightly out of breath.

"You're late." Grace declared crossly and folded her arms.

Colin laughed and pulled the young girl towards him and kissed her fondly, "Sorry darling. I had things to finish."

"You finish at five, what did you have to finish?"

"Invoices my sweet. Are we going in then?"

The wind was picking up and blew coldly against her cheeks, she could stay out here and argue, but a warm pub with a hot fire sounded very inviting so she numbly nodded, "Yes. Lou will be wondering about me."

Colin walked slightly in front and pulled the door towards them and waved an arm to Grace to let her through first. She stepped over the welcome mat and the noisy din that reverberated in the tavern suddenly came to a close. The whole place was silent as many eyes and heads turned to watch and follow them as they made their way over to where Grace's friends were sitting. She sat down self-consciously and was very unsure what to say, she knew she didn't come out often but the way the locals stared made her paranoid.

"I'll get us some drinks. Lemonade and vodka Grace?" Colin asked and before waiting for a response, made his way over to the bar.

"Why are they staring at me that way? Is it because they haven't seen me in a long time? Do they feel sorry for me? What is it?" Grace questioned her friends, wiggling out of her coat aware that everyone was watching. She knew deep down this was a bad idea, she should never have come.

"Oh, Gracie it's not that. It's…" Lou began, unsure what to say next.

"Come on. We need to go. Let's head back to my place, it's not far thankfully." Ian continued for Lou.

"Good idea Ian. It's better for Gracie that way. Come on Gracie, quickly get your coat back on."

Obediently Grace shrugged her coat back on and was just about to follow Ian and Lou out of the back door when a man shouted behind her. A smash from a bottle or pint glass shattered the silence and many men stood up to face the bar. Grace could see Colin slightly waving his arms up and down, trying to soothe the mob that came closer to him. She could hear his coaxing voice crying out, "Fella's! Fella's! Can't have a guy have a drink with his girl and her friends?"

"She's not your girl. And you're not welcome here," snarled the barman barring his teeth and giving Colin an evil look. "You're banned remember. Now you better leave before the cops get here."

"Cops," Colin smirked and laughed loudly, "What cops? Ryans and Edmonds? They're so slow they can't even catch a bus!"

"Then you'll have us to deal with!" A man called out from somewhere amongst the crowd.

"Grace is one of ours! You swine! She is not some whore you can pick up from the alleys of St

Louisham! Go back to where you came from!" The barman reached for a shotgun he kept above the counter and filled it with shells and clicked the machine into place and aimed it at Colin, "She is ready and loaded. Now. What'll it be?"

Colin continued to smile, "Easy Murphy. Do you even know how to use that thing?"

More smashes were heard as the group of men broke their beer bottles and pointed the sharp ends towards him. A murmur came across the place, Grace held her breath paralysed to the core and unable to move. The seconds on the clock by the bar ticked by loudly. A whole minute passed.

"You win Murphy." Colin responded and threw his hands up, "You bloody win."

And with that he grabbed his coat, slung it over one shoulder and left the pub, once again all eyes were on Grace. Grace was uncontrollably sobbing on Lou's shoulder,

"What happened?" she wept, pressing a damp handkerchief to her face. "I don't understand."

"Lou. She needs to know," said Ian, glancing at his girlfriend. She nodded slowly and quietly, Ian took Lou by the hand and lead her out of the back, Grace subduedly followed.

They headed quickly down the main street silently, none of them looked at each other or said a word. The full moon peered out of the clouds and radiated its cold light on the village, lighting up the eerie shadows on the dark corners. There were no streetlights on the road they turned down on, just pitch darkness, punctuated now and again by a light from someone's window. They must have reached their destination because Ian suddenly crouched down by some hedges and beckoned the girls to do likewise. Grace watched spellbound unsure what she was supposed to be seeing. Unless they were meeting someone? She trusted Lou and Ian and felt safe pressed in the middle of them. A low humming noise met her ears as a tall dark figure waltzed right pass them, she crouched down further even though there was no chance of being seen. A small light by a house 100 yards in front of them came on and an extremely loud knock on the door almost made her jump. It was a few moments before the door swung open, and a female silhouette stood in the doorway,

"What the hell are you doing? What's wrong with you? Stupid man!"

"Nice night. Been to the pub."

"Yeah? Well, you don't stink of beer you liar, where's the bimbo? You woke up Emily, so you'd better get in and get her back to sleep. Her screaming will wake the dead if you don't hurry up."

The door banged shut and the peacefulness of nature once more took over, an owl flew by hooting to its mate and getting a clear response. Grace looked at

Lou and she knew that she knew, unable to keep back the tears she left and went home.

*

The next morning was a gloomier day, the rain poured, and the tears poured. Grace couldn't face her parents that morning, so she spent most of her time in her room, drawing meaningless pictures in her scrapbook. She couldn't face talking to Colin either, not after finding out what kind of a man he really was. He was so perfect, so charming, attractive, kind and incredibly patient with her, happily waiting for days if not weeks to see her. It now made more sense to her why he was so happy to wait, probably had a couple of girls on the side. She felt like a fool, how could she have been such an imbecile.

"Grace?" Her mother called from downstairs, "Someone here to see you."

Grace looked out of her bedroom window saw her visitor and sighed, "Coming Mama."

She splashed water on her face, tidied her hair and smoothed down her dress and tried her best to smile. With a heavy heart she left her room and made her way to the front door which was already open.

"Hello Nathan."

"Grace. Lou told me." Nathan began, for once in his life he was speechless. Grace assumed he was also in shock by her own foolishness, she expected him to give her a good talk on her stupidity. She was surprised when he said, "I have some flowers for you. Fresh from Daisy's in St Heliers."

Grace took the flowers and smelled them, "Thank you Nathan. I'm touched."

Nathan nodded, "I just want to say, I'm sorry. I knew you and Colin were together, I accidently overheard a few times when you were telephoning."

Grace looked at him suspiciously. Knowing Nathan, there was no, so called 'accident,' just plain old eavesdropping, she said, "It's ok Nathan. Really, I'm fine."

"You probably wish you went out with me now. That Colin, the dirty cheat. I should have given him a black eye when I had the chance. It's a wonder his wife lets him home."

Grace looked at him and wondered if she was the only person in Morecombe who didn't realise he was married with a family. She had spent a lot of time at St Heliers college training to be a teacher and living with a dear friend meant she was a lot of the time away from home.

"So," Nathan continued, looking down and shuffled his feet, "Do you want to go for a drink sometime next week? You can try doubles again. You know me, and you know I'm not attached to anyone. I've only ever had eyes for you Grace darling."

Grace wondered why he just called her darling, she responded, "I'll think about it and let you know. I need time."

A loud shout bellowed from the upstairs window, "GRACE! I can hear you and that boy talking. I told you to GET RID OF HIM!"

"Sorry Nathan," Grace quietly uttered, closing her eyes for a second in disbelief at the manners of her father and sighed, "You should go. It's best if you don't come over, my father, he…"

"He is a rude old man with no manners." Nathan finished for her and walked off shutting the gate surprisingly gentle. Grace almost laughed out loud as Nathan described himself exactly to a tee, rude and with no manners! Even though he was understandable compassionate and kind just now which made for a nice change.

They left it at that, Nathan went about his day and Grace feeling slightly fresher went to do some gardening. The weeds were uncontrollably getting taller, and the grass needed a good cut, maybe I could do some hanging baskets with petunias she thought to herself.

Chapter 6
Present Day

Following on from my discussion with Linda, the woman living at The Pines. I decided she was right on one thing; Roger knew a lot more about the neighbours at The Larches than he was letting on. It was time I paid him another visit. And that's where I found myself a few hours later, sitting on the red settee once more, eyeing the cuckoo clock and wondering when it would pop out. The dogs come blundering in, saliva drooling from their mouths as they jumped up at me barking excitedly.

"Down boy!" I said, using my sternest voice and gave the Labradors a gentle but firm nudge. They soon took heed and ran back to the kitchen as the sound of dog food rattled into a tin bowl. Diana Hope appeared around the corner with a tray consisting of a pot of tea, cups and saucers and some Victoria sponge. She delicately served me a cup and she must have assumed I was a man with a hearty stomach for she gave me a large wedge of cake. She picked up her knitting bag and exited the room.

"Hello sir. This looks rather jolly. Diana has seen to you I see." A man called out from the doorway he was standing in and ambled slowly to an armchair and helped himself to morning tea.

"Good to see you again Roger. Hope you don't mind me dropping in?" I said, digging my fork into the sponge.

"No. I enjoy company. Unfortunately, you see less and less people as you get older. People just don't seem interested anymore. So, what brings you to my humble abode? Another suspicious death?"

"Well sort of." I muttered, unsure where to start on the topic, "I'm investigating the house next door."

"What? Linda and Arthur Storm's place? They are an eccentric couple I suppose, always coming and going. Linda can easily talk the hind leg of a donkey if not all the legs! Now don't say one of them has been murdered!"

"No, no Roger. I mean the house at the end, The Larches."

"Oh. That place. We don't talk about that place. I told you before, it's evil." Roger looked away from me and stared at his hot cup of tea and carefully took a sip. For a few minutes we concentrated on eating our cake in complete silence.

Delicately I broke the ice, "I don't want to talk about the house. I want to know about the people who lived there. I already saw Michael yesterday who mentioned his father, Nathan Barnes. And a few of the local residents remember Michael's mother, Grace. There was another child, a girl. Laura or Lauren?"

"Lydia. Yes, Michael and Grace's daughter, she is the oldest of the lot. So beautiful, like her mother. Long brown hair, brown hazel eyes that could melt your heart, a smile to warm your soul. Ah yes, she was a stunner. She lives in the village now, divorced but still goes by the name of Sawyers. I'll get Diana to write her address."

"There were four of them. Is that right?"

"Four children? Yes, that's right. After Lydia there was Jacob. Poor sod, he was only eighteen years old, just had his birthday. I believe it was his dad Michael who found the poor beggar. He was fixing a combine harvester, wasn't propelling forwards properly or something according to one of the farmhands. Next thing he was crushed underneath it. I helped to get him out, but the damage was done. Grace was distraught poor thing, don't think she ever recovered. Lydia's divorce came through the year after which really broke Grace's heart. And then there's Michael as you know, took over the farm from Jeff and Susan Jackson. His wife left him too, took both kids with her. And lastly there's Sofie, breast cancer I think is what took her, she died last year."

"A lot of bad luck in that family." I mumbled, placing my empty cup on the tray. "So did you work for Nathan?"

"I worked with him, not for him. That man was bloody useless for someone who'd supposedly worked there all of his adult life. Couldn't tell the difference between grains or had the know how when a cow was about to give birth. Michael, now he's a good farmer. Unfortunately, he is so rude and upsets a lot of the labourers, most of them have left to find work elsewhere." Roger poured me out another cup of tea and continued, "Grace has died now. You'll find her in St Lukes Churchyard, along with her son. Nathan is in a retirement home in St Louisham, lost his marbles poor boy. Rambling on about all sorts of stuff and nonsense. It's the best place for him to be honest. I was a very young boy in those days, used to visit the farm and earn my tuppence, but I still remember Nathan very well. He used to skive off and visit Grace, break into her house and wait for her to return just so he can talk to her. He was a law breaker unto himself, went well out of his way just to woo the girl and offer her a hand in marriage. There was a time quite a bit later, when Grace was seeing an unsatisfactory man, very unpopular in Morecombe. Nathan had overheard the telephone call and rallied the locals together to form a mob and spring an attack on that man. Just shows how far Nathan will go for Grace, wooed her with flowers the very next morning!"

I sat back on the sofa wondering to myself if it was Colin Marsh that Roger was mentioning? Ann did mention her father dating Grace at one point.

"What was the name of Grace's parents?" I suddenly asked, full of curiosity. "The ones that…well. You know…"

"Yes, I know too well young man," said Roger, clearing his throat, "They'll be in the graveyard too. Elsie and John Forrester. It was a beautiful send off, I remember it like yesterday."

"Do you have any idea who did it?"

"None whatsoever."

*

After my morning tea session at Roger and Diana Hope's house I had two choices to make, find Lydia or find the graves. The sun was beaming down strongly, and the wind had ceased to blow, a very pleasant afternoon to saunter amongst gravestones. St Lukes Church wasn't large in size nor the graveyard that lay around it, none of the graves were brand new, most of them were covered in moss and lichen. They were scattered about haphazardly in no particular order, which made the search harder and some of the stones had eroded away leaving no name behind. A white angel sat on a small square marble block which had a plaque bearing the name:

Colin Andrew Marsh
Died Aged 62
1925-1988
May you rest in peace

I thought to myself that an angel chosen was extremely cynical, from what he had heard of the villagers, Colin Marsh was no angel. I headed up the slope and round the back of the Church and was surprised to see fresh roses on four of the tombstones.

They were all lined up together in a row covered in ivy that crept over the wall, two of the stones looked slighter newer than the others. I steadily approached the first stone which looked newest:

Grace Alice Barnes
Died Aged 56
1937-1993
May your soul be truly rested

It came as no surprise to read the stone next to hers was her son who tragically died so young.

Jacob Barnes
Died Aged 18
1962-1980
Almost a man and yet never forgotten

What a waste of a life. Health and safety this day and age would never let such a thing happen. The other two stones which were looking slightly weathered and tired contained what I knew to be, Elisa and John Forrester. Calculating the dates, they were both in their early sixties when the event unfolded in 1958, Grace must have been in her early twenties. I wondered to myself, who could have done this? And why? The why question was bothering me the most, an old couple both of ill health just keeping to themselves and not upsetting anyone. What was the purpose of their murder? What was there to gain? There was no sign of Grace's daughter Sophie, she must have been buried in the newer cemetery outside of the village. A really unlucky family, bad luck seemed to follow them wherever they went, from Grace's parents to Grace's own children and possibly grandchildren. I decided it was time I went and found Lydia and see if she could add anything to the story.

*

Her house was again another easy house to find, pastel pink with a dark pink door and windows and autumn annuals blooming from the plant boxes. I knocked several times but to no avail, I stood pondering on my next move.

"She's out," said a face popping out of the window next door, "She'll be at the café."

I thanked her and walked briskly back to the high street, almost laughing and thought how amazing it was that the people I was interested in were so close together. The café was steamy inside and busy, only by chance I found a chair by the window.

"Well now. Lovely to see you again," cooed Linda, and poured me a hot coffee, "Did you go and find Roger? Hasn't he got a lot to say? Knows all about that family as I told you, he was a close friend of Nathan's, best friends more like. Are you anywhere closer to finding out who did it? I bet my cards it was that Colin Marsh bloke, the way these old people harp on about him. Have you spoken to Ann? Ann can tell you a lot about him and her old biddys. They swear it was him and by the sounds of it he's more than likely to have done it, vicious temper apparently! And seeing all the local ladies on the side, upsetting their families; his own family included! Unfortunately, I haven't lived here long enough so what happened back then is just as mysterious to me as it is to you. When you do find the killer, please let me know and give me all the details!"

I smiled and agreed, "Is Lydia here?"

"Course she is. This café used to be hers you know until she semi-retired, she still hasn't left the place. Her husband bought the place as a divorce present would you believe, deliberately made the whole place grey with white and black furniture. It looked like a black and white photo when I saw the picture, Lydia soon saw to that and added colour. To be honest it was extremely generous of him, could've left her out to dry. She's done rather well for herself and her daughter. That's Lydia over there by the counter. Do you think she is a suspect? Hang on no, that's impossible she wasn't even born then! I got it, you think Grace has something to do with it and Lydia might know something more about her mother than she's letting on. I'll let you guys have tea in the back room, give you some space to chat. So exciting! LYDIA!"

A tall slim woman with streaky grey lines in her brunette hair glided over towards them, she was smiling a smile that made you feel warm inside. Her face looked only slightly wrinkled with age and yet her eyes were still young as ever. Roger was right, she was a stunner.

"Lydia, this is Tom," Linda said and then whispered, "He's a detective."

"It's ok Linda. Word of Detective Inspector Tom Jones has got around. So, what are you investigating now? I assume you're no longer looking into that girl who fell of the cliff since it was clearly an accident. Have you started a new investigation then? I overheard you two talking about the murders of Mr and Mrs Forrester, aka my grandparents. You won't find who did it, it's been the village mystery for more than sixty years."

"I'm determined to try. I was hoping you could give me some information on your parents and family life in general," I explained, following her into the room at the back, which had two chairs lying haphazardly and plenty of magazines scattered over a little table. Lydia pulled the chairs across to the table and shoved the magazines onto a crammed bookshelf.

"Gosh. Sounds like an interrogation!" She exclaimed and sat down, crossing her legs and folding her arms.

"Not at all, I was hoping we could talk as friends. If that is alright?"

Linda came in with hot coffee and Viennese swirls and answered for Lydia, "Course we can all talk as friends. We want to find the killer, don't we Lydia? Even if he is long dead and buried which is probably the case!"

"Or she." I said, thinking of Grace as I dipped a swirl into my cup. "Killer could be a she."

"No. It's definitely a he, can you see a woman with a shotgun killing a couple in cold blood? I can't."

"Who are your suspects?" Lydia asked, leaning forward slightly. "Apart from Colin, the local outlaw of his time which the whole village knows about. I can give you another suspect, my father."

Me and Linda were stunned to hear Lydia mention her own father as a possible murderer, we just looked at each other shocked. Linda muttered she had customers to serve and left me and Lydia to it.

Lydia continued undisturbed by her statement, "You didn't know my father as well as I did. Mother always sang his praises, how he was there for her at times of trouble, a charming man who frequently bought her presents. But I heard the arguments and I saw the marks on her body the next day. Cat and dog, they were. He worked at the farm stupid long hours. I hardly saw him growing up. Mother raised us and did her best, constantly he found fault and it upset him when things didn't go his way and he always blamed her."

"What made you assume he could be the killer?" I inquired.

"Well recently he has been diagnosed with dementia, he's still in the early stages so there are times when he knows what he's doing and saying. I dropped him off at the residential home last month and something he said got me really upset. He said…well he didn't say as such. He was actually laughing when he said,

'Did you see their bloody faces? Nothing left of them.' I couldn't believe what I just heard, the way he referred to my grandparents. Honestly, I believe it was him and if it wasn't him, then he at least had something to do with it."

I paused thoughtfully, there could be something in that, "He must have been there when it happened. Do you know who called the police?"

"No idea," said Lydia, suddenly looking tired. "I wasn't born then, most of what I know came from my mother Grace. She was nearing the end when we finally got talking truthfully about matters past."

"Did she say anything important that could help find who did it?"

"Yes…I think. There was one more thing. Don't know if it's important. No, it's not important, just idle talk."

"What was?"

"She said something like, 'It's the curse. Me and Nathan, when we were young. We found a box and opened it and he said the words. How were we to know it was cursed. We left the box behind where it will never be found.' Mother has a picture of a strange girl in her house too. Michael still has it I think, he didn't change the house at all after mother died and father left."

"Where's the box now? Did you look for it after that talk with your mother?"

"No. I don't know where the box is," muttered Lydia letting off a deep sigh, "But…I don't think it's ever left the location where it was found. It's still there at that house. The Larches."

The Larches. The bloody Larches! I exclaimed to myself in annoyance. Why did everything lead back to that house! What was going on at that place?

"I'm afraid I've got nothing more to add. Michael probably knows more, unfortunately he is disagreeable. Doesn't enjoy people coming over, he is extremely rude too," said Lydia, standing up to end our meeting, "I've got to get back. Can't let Linda do all the work."

"One more thing," I stammered, standing up hurriedly to stop her for a minute from leaving, "Can you come with me to see Michael? He might be more open and comfortable if you were there. And I don't know how to talk to him on my own."

"Ok. I'll arrange something and let you know. You're staying at The Red Lobster, aren't you? I'll find you there."

Linda might have had customers to serve, yet it didn't stop her hovering near the door and listen in when she had the opportunity. She must have overheard a lot for she gave both of us a very beady look and followed Lydia across the room. I said my goodbyes and had almost left when Linda placed a hand on the door,

"How long are you at The Red Lobster till?"

"Tomorrow." I replied, pulling on some warm gloves.

"That must be very expensive for you! Listen, me and Arthur we have a spare room you can use, no excuses! And it's right next door to your house! It's very costly at the pub, Brian charges a fortune, and it's sounds like you'll be here for a while yet. Come round tomorrow at 6pm, the room will be ready then. Then you can fill us in and maybe me and Arthur can help you with your investigation. We don't know the village very well, but we hear a lot from our customers and the gossip round here will burn your ears!"

"Well thank you very much Linda. You're very kind."

"Don't mention it. I'll need to let Arthur know first," she responded with a twinkle in her eye and a large grin on her face. She closed the door firmly behind me as I wondered to myself, what now?

Chapter 7

The next morning, I ventured into Morecombe once more and decided to pay a visit to Constable Jonathan Jack to give him an update on events and see if he had anything to add. A double possible homicide in a small village was incredibly rare, so there must be something in the police files. The police house was unusually quiet, hardly a squeak or a small murmur of talk or noise of any sort. Jacks was busy at his desk scribbling on a piece of paper with his illegible handwriting. A large untidy pile lay next to him, whether they were waiting to be completed or were already completed I couldn't decide, I called out to him,

"Morning Jacks!"

"Jones! How are you?" Jacks replied, pushing his chair back and clicking his pen before throwing it down. "How's it going with the Jenny case?"

"Nothing there. Accident, I'm almost certain. Roger only saw the one light, if there was more than one person there would be more than one light in that fog. Nothing to show there was another person there. Then again, I could be wrong, Sean Conway wasn't helpful in the slightest, slammed the door right into my face!"

"Bruised ego that one. He knows something and it's chewing him up in guilt. Only the guilty people either cower behind closed doors or behave bold as brass with a smug look on their face."

"I've started a new investigation which might have something to do with Jenny's death. The Larches." I explained and was about to take a seat when the door crashed behind me.

"Morning all." Called a deep gruff voice. A burly police officer walked in and took his place behind the reception desk and read the local paper whilst sipping a hot coffee.

"Don't mind Dave. He has the most boring job in the whole village," Jacks whispered and answered my statement in a normal voice, "The Larches? Derelict house near to where Jenny died? What about it?"

"The couple living there in 1958 were Elsie and John Forrester, both in their sixties, shot close range in the head. Their daughter was a girl called Grace, married a man called Nathan Barnes. They had four children, Michael lives at the farm, Lydia works at the café." I announced, taking the police constable by surprise.

Constable Jack gave a long whistle, "Hardly surprising that the house has been left in such a state! I assume you've been talking to the locals?"

I continued my statement, "No-one was caught although Colin Marsh was arrested and released. Lydia thinks it could be her father, Nathan."

"Of course it was Colin Marsh!" said a growly voice behind me, placing down a cup of coffee in front of me. "Everyone who lives here knows it was him. Bloody coward got away with it, carried on his bigamist ways and moved in with a girlfriend shortly after."

"It was never proven Dave. He could be innocent." Jacks piped up, giving me a side look and raised his eyes.

"Nope. It was Colin Marsh. End of investigation!"

I ignored him, I was too deep into this investigation to conclude it was Colin Marsh, as Jacks said, there was no evidence, no actual proof. The policemen of that time had released him based on no evidence, which must be a sign of his innocence surely?

Jacks asked curiously, "Did you find out anything else?"

"Nothing more to add," I replied, placing my coffee down in disgust, "There was a young boy who died there, but I need to ask Ann or Nigel Fern more questions."

Dave guffawed loudly, spluttering on his hot drink, "You're interviewing the vicar? Do you suspect then that he could be possibly hiding a shotgun up his cassock? Or something more sinister…like a Mars Bar in the middle of a service for instance? Whichever it is, I hope he's confessed his sins!"

I stood solemnly giving the big man a cold stare, I didn't approve of this kind of humour against the local vicar, "Nigel Fern was only a child at the time. So, there would be no reason for him to have a shotgun or fire it or let alone hide one on his persons."

"Lighten up Jones, just a bit of banter," muttered Dave and returned to his newspaper.

"Right, I've got to carry on with my reports for the last few days. Bit behind as you can see." Constable Jack turned around and returned to his table and picked up his discarded pen and bid me good day.

Once outside I decided to also buy a local paper from the post office, see what rumours might have been spreading around the small village. After a quick glance over I was slightly disappointed and yet relieved to see there was nothing of interest. The bus turned up punctual and I took a return to St Louisham.

*

St Louisham retirement home was a short walk away from the town along the coastal path, which was mostly a few miles of road along the seafront. It was another pleasant autumn day, a few small fishing boats bobbed up and down on the water, the fishermen sat perfectly still and waited with intense patience. Two small dogs barked and raced with one another along the shore, skidding on the loose pebbles and sending the stones flying backwards. A young couple embracing against the cold wind, looked on at the dogs and called them to heel, before venturing off in the opposite direction.

The home was an impressive Victorian building with many floors and windows looking out onto different scenes of life. Its brown and orange hue was a strong contrast against the green fields and grey cliffs in the background. Various flower arrangements lined every windowsill and hanging baskets hung by the main door. A few elderly people in wheelchairs and blankets sat under a veranda attached to the side of the building, ensuring that they got the best of all weathers, rain or sun. I ambled through the main door and found myself in a small room with a large welcome desk which took up half the room itself. A large vase of lilies half blocked my view of the receptionist, the smell from the flowers was intoxicating and made my head feel giddy.

"Good morning, sir. Can I help?" The lady asked, not looking up from her computer as she hammered away at the keyboard.

"Yes," I answered, unravelling several layers as a found myself sweating in the stuffy room, "I'm looking for Nathan Barnes."

"Mr Barnes? Of course. I'll just get someone up to his room and see if he's ready for a visitor. You really should have rung first. Nathan Barnes doesn't like visitors." She abruptly said and looked at me for a quick brief second. The receptionist stood up, smoothed down her short skirt and left the room for a minute, she soon returned and reassumed her position at the desk. I leaned awkwardly against the counter admiring the place, before venturing around the room and glimpsing into other rooms.

"Hello sir. You're here to see Mr Barnes?" A young boy questioned, appearing from nowhere it seemed, I puzzled on which room he came from.

"Yes," I answered, wondering how much longer this will take.

"He's ready to see you. If you can fill in the visitor book, please. Veronica will take your details."

After spending several more minutes faffing over a few silly forms, we ventured upstairs to the top floor and along a corridor which had a panoramic view of the sea and town from its long horizontal windows. The lad knocked on the door labelled Nathan Barnes,

"Mr Barnes? Your visitor."

A mumble could be heard from the other side of the door, the boy opened it and let me in, before swiftly exiting. An elderly man sat in a wicker armchair full of cushions, a rug was pulled up snuggly to his bristled chin. He was almost completely bald, save for a few short white whispery hairs that stuck up in random places, his hands were thin and bony and covered in warts. When he looked up at me, his eyes were a watery pale blue on his wrinkled face and when he talked, I noticed a few teeth were missing.

"Thomas Jones," he softly murmured and waved a trembling hand towards a chair opposite, "Do I know you? I don't remember your name."

"No, you don't know me." I answered.

"What?" Nathan asked and held a hand to his ear, so I repeated my sentence a little louder, Nathan continued, "What brings you here then?"

"I have a few questions to ask. When you were younger. When you and Grace first met."

"I see. You want to know about my family and my wife. Grace is dead now, almost twenty years ago. Not a day goes by when I don't think about her."

I thought to myself whether what he said could be true. As a man who beat his wife, surely he can't miss her that much?

Nathan coughed a horrid mucus cough, "Tell me what you know. And I'll tell you what you don't know."

He laid back into his chair placing one arm over the other and closed his eyes, as I retold my story as much as I could remember, leaving out all the nasty things that were said about Nathan.

Nathan opened his eyes and looked at me, smirking slightly, "You seem to know a lot about my family. Fascinating case, aren't we? Roger knows so much…too much it seems. He was my best friend. We don't talk as much as we used too. I lost my son you know. He was the best son a man could have, loved that boy so much. Unlike Michael, who could love him? Such an aggressive nasty little child and then one day he turned into a horrid ignorant man. I would keep my distance if I was you."

I was uncomfortable the way he talked about his son in such a brutal manner, "Have I covered everything?"

"You have indeed." Nathan replied calmly and shut his eyes once more and appeared to be falling asleep.

"I'll leave you then. I appreciate you seeing me." I said, feeling defeated and raised from my chair, grabbing my various pieces of clothing.

"Did you see her?" Nathan quietly asked without moving or opening his eyes.

"What?"

"Did you see her? The girl who lives at The Larches."

"No-one lives there Mr Barnes. It's been deserted and left at it was since Mr and Mrs Forrester died."

Nathan chuckled in a sinister fashion and suddenly wheezed hysterically before pressing a red button by his bed. I decided it was best to leave, having no longer a desire to be in the same room as him.

*

It was quieter in town, now that the day was drawing to a close. I saw Brian Fletcher standing outside of The Three Kings, a tavern full of noisy people that was getting louder by the minute. It was a dismal pub lurking on the corner of an alleyway, it's walls and windows were blackened with soot from the carbon that hung in the air. There was no splash of colour apart from a circus poster in the window dated five years ago. The door of the place crashed open as a group of men fell out and spilled onto the street, causing several cars to brake and hoot in alarm. A picnic bench got broken in the scuffle as punches were thrown and a man got pushed backwards, sending pint glasses flying. A tall man with the thickest muscles I had ever seen emerged from the doorway and separated the men. It turned out to be just the one man who had caused the trouble, as he spat out a few more curse words to the men walking away. Brian was still standing in the same spot, miraculously unscathed and smoking a cigarette. I looked on as he helped the young lad stand up unsteadily, onto his feet and pressed the glass of ice he was holding against his forehead. I soon recognised the lad as Sean Conway, the ex-boyfriend of Jenny Hops and main suspect in her death. Brian was giving him a good talking to, but I couldn't hear from where I was stood so I cautiously headed over.

"And look who it is. Stalking me, are we?" Sean stuttered, his bloody lip giving him trouble to speak properly. He motioned to move away from me and then with a groan he grabbed his ribs.

Brian launched forward to catch him and helped him sit on a bench by the main entrance, "You should go to hospital Sean. Get the once over."

"Hate hospitals," he replied drunkenly and shrugged the man off, "They'll keep me there for days."

"So? Not like you're doing much with your spare time is it?"

"What job is it that you do Mr Conway?" I asked, sitting down at the other end of the bench.

"Mr Conway? Bit la-di-da, aren't you? Posh guy from the big city? I know your type! It's Sean to you and I'm at university in St Heliers." Sean retorted spitting out blood into the glass of ice he was holding before placing it back on his head.

"What are you studying Sean?"

"Paranormal Science and Ufology. I'm working towards my Parapsychology degree."

"Wow! Sounds impressive."

Sean looked at me with slightly less contempt and almost managed a small smile, "Well…thanks. You know, that's how me and Jenny met, we were studying the same thing. She was more interested than I was, got her degree long before I did. I failed the first time, so I'll be trying again later at the end of the summer term."

"I'm just going in to get us some more pints. You want one Tom?" Brian asked.

I nodded to Brian before turning back to Sean, "Were you and Jenny close? I heard she was staying with you at the time of the accident."

"So, you know it was an accident and that I didn't have anything to do with it? I told Jacks, he wouldn't believe me," Sean paused to receive the fresh full glass Brian was holding out to him, "I told her not to go up there. She was fascinated with a paranormal case she had been reading, got it into her head that the house was haunted."

"The Larches?"

"The Larches. Paranormal investigators headed up that way last year, wrote a blog on their website. It was literally on our doorstep and Jenny couldn't resist so she headed over there that night. The only thing she didn't account for was the fog, takes you unaware it does, I assume she got lost in the fog and fell."

I agreed with him and took a swig, "Have you been up there?"

"Me? No. I don't want to now, if Jenny was with me, I probably would go. Don't want to look chicken."

I dug into my coat pocket and pulled out some jewellery, "Did this bracelet belong to Jenny?"

"Yes. I gave it to Jenny for her 21st birthday." Sean said, gently taking it from my fingers and placing it in his hand, "Where was it?"

"At the house. It was on the floor. The link has broken off, you can see it's snapped in two."

"I saw it in the window of the pawnshop down the road, I was surprised to find out it was Michael's, he lives at Morecombe Farm. Said it belongs to his wife, she left him you see, so he was getting rid of all the things she left behind. Including that bracelet."

There was slight pause as we drank our drinks in silence, the street was completely empty by now.

"One more question Sean." I said, placing my empty glass down, "How did she get a bruise on her jaw?"

Sean shifted himself uncomfortably, "You wouldn't believe me."

Brian interrupted, "I can vouch for that. They were in my pub playing pool, Sean swung his cue stick round and accidently clonked her on the chin."

"Satisfied Detective?"

I wasn't satisfied yet I hesitantly bobbed my head, "Thank you. Yes, I'm satisfied."

"Right. Home for you Sean. You're going to have a wicked hangover in the morning. Best get some rest." Brian announced and helped him to stand up.

"Please don't go and recommend coconut water before bed! Or camomile tea! Hate the stuff!"

I took Sean's other arm and together we slowly stumbled towards Brian's car, which was inconveniently parked on the other side of town. I was thoroughly exhausted by the time we got back and dropped Sean off. Brian and myself headed back to the pub, I gathered the rest of my belongings and said farewell to Brian, knowing that in such a small village we'll probably see each other quite soon!

Dusk was setting in quickly, which only just gave me enough time to walk up the coastal path towards the Storms place. The Pines was lit up in a sunset sky of gold, the windows shimmered, and the few dimmed solar lights positioned around the house came on. The garden was mainly laid to lawn, with the exception of a few pine trees which lined the right side of the house when looking at it from the gate. It was dead on 6pm as I made my way around the side of the building and knocked on the door. The door was opened with such vigour whilst I was knocking that I almost fell through the doorway.

"Tom! You made it! So good to see you again. Arthur!"

"Hello Linda," I responded, pecking her powdered cheek and followed her through into a spacious hallway.

"This is Arthur," she said lovingly with pride in her voice, "He's a car salesman in St Louisham. Awfully good at his job! Thanks to him, we can live here."

"I was in St Louisham today. Visiting someone and then bumping into another person."

"Ooh! Please tell me you were interviewing more suspects! Ooh I can't wait to hear everything. Now start from the beginning. Arthur will get the drinks!"

The next few hours passed pleasantly, Linda had cooked a supreme roast chicken with baby potatoes and steamed veg, all swimming in gravy. Followed by a luxurious sponge pudding with custard. We discussed the investigation with detail, I made sure to include everything and leave nothing out. Linda's eyes opened more and more as the tale got juicier and spookier by the minute.

"So, the house is haunted? Is that what's been said?" She asked, reflecting for a moment to let the story sink in. "To think Arthur, that we live next door to a haunted house! Who did it Tom?"

"If I knew that I would tell you. At the moment it's either Colin Marsh or Nathan Barnes. Haven't got any other suspects." I answered, accepting another cup of filter coffee.

"Who's the girl Nathan mentioned?" Arthur asked curiously.

"No idea. I don't even know if there is a girl! What strikes me odd is that Nathan hasn't been back to that place since Grace's parents died. Obviously, the girl was there then, although she can no longer be a girl anymore, more likely to be an elderly lady if she is still alive that is. Why did Nathan ask if I've seen a girl there? Doesn't make sense."

"You're forgetting he has dementia. Poor old man. He was probably asking you a question thinking it was the fifties."

"You're probably right," I said, still feeling unsure, my head was pounding and feeling extremely sore. Linda must have seen me rubbing my tired eyes as she suddenly jumped up and said, 'Bedtime.'

I was offered a comfortable looking room full of pink, a pink fluffy bed sat on a pale pink fluffy carpet with pink curtains to match the pink walls. Fortunately, the furniture around was mostly white. Next Linda showed me the bathroom which was also white and had fluffy towels and a fluffy bathmat. I smiled at her eccentricity and bade her goodnight and turned into my room for the night.

It was past two in the morning when I woke up suddenly with a start, it took me a while to gather my bearings and remember where I was. I lay there for a while, wondering why I was awake. I was almost asleep again when I heard a creaking noise from outside, silently I peered out of the curtains and noticed the garden gate was open. It was swinging back and forth on its hinges. I was so sure I had closed it and slid the bolt home when I came through earlier. Suddenly I noticed a dark shadowy figure by the gate, having emerged from behind the hedge from where they were standing. I watched intrigued wondering what this person was doing hovering around so late at night. They stood awhile before heading further up the coastal path in the opposite direction to the village. The next thing I heard was the back door clicking open and a light streamed onto the lawn, Arthur Storm waded through the thick grass and closed the gate promptly. I heard Linda call out, but I couldn't catch what she said. The door closed and I heard them climb the stairs and retreat to bed themselves. If it wasn't Linda or Arthur hanging around the bottom of the garden. Who was?

Chapter 8
1958

April weather was at its fullest, warm sunshine one minute and heavy showers the next. Grace was calmly knitting a red jumper, sitting on the window seat and watching the rain splash on the glass. The clouds grew darker and rumbled, the girl watched expectantly for a flash of lightning which sadly didn't happen. A loud rap on the front door made her jump and drop a few stitches, she sighed crossly and ignored the visitor who had just rudely ruined her knitting. The knocking continued louder and more urgently, not wanting her parents to wake up she decided to answer the door.

"Lou!" Grace exclaimed and pulled her friend inside, "What are you doing? It's raining cats and dogs out there!"

Lou struggled out of her wet coat that was clinging to her body and removed her soaked shoes. Grace promptly gave her a towel to dry her wet hair and proceeded into the next room to light the fire. Soon the flames were roaring and burning up the dry logs at speed, the girls drank hot tea and dunked in digestives.

"Sorry to burst in on you Gracie. It started to rain, and your house was the nearest. It was sunny when I left Ian's."

"Well, that must have been ages ago, it's been raining nonstop for an hour already!" said Grace.

Lou looked put out and stroked her hair off her forehead, "Ian has asked me to marry him."

Grace gave a radiating smile and reached out to her friend, "That's wonderful news!"

"Is it? I didn't give him an answer, I just made an excuse and left."

"Why Lou? You and Ian are perfect for each other. You've been together for several years, and I know how much Ian cares for you and you for him."

"Oh Gracie. I'm usually so good in situations and resolving them. Why can't I this once make up my mind," Lou sighed and pulled a plump cushion to her chest.

"It's a big decision. Till death do us part. Do you want to be with Ian till you die?" Grace asked.

"Of course, I do…at the moment. But what if something goes wrong? What if…"

"Lou. All marriages have their ups and downs, something will go wrong, but things will go right too. Forget about the what if's and worrying about the future and concentrate on the now and enjoy every day of it."

Lou gave a small smile and looked at Grace, "You know. You can be very wise when you want to be."

"Not all the time. I messed up with Colin and now Nathan is on my back." Grace exhaled deeply.

"Nathan Barnes. The idiot working for Jeff Jackson at the farm?"

"Yes, that one."

"Urgh. He creeps me out, not sure why. The way he looks at you and the way he's just…well…there! Right there in your face! I wouldn't be surprised if he was outside right now!"

A loud rumble of thunder sounded above the house and a loud bang and flash of lightning lit the blackened sky. The lights fizzled and with a quiet pop went out, leaving the room in almost complete darkness if it hadn't been for the fire. Both girls leapt up, spilling the plate of biscuits lying precariously on the table, and held each other's hands in the dark.

"It's just the electrics," Grace gasped, catching her breath as her heart rate slowed down. They both glanced at each other and laughed, knowing that they were both being very silly over a thunderstorm. Grace found a torch by the kitchen counter, donned her mackintosh and wellies and headed outside,

"I won't be long. The electricity box is round the side of the house in the cellar." Grace explained and closed the back door firmly.

Lou waited impatiently, tapping her foot and bobbed up and down on the spot, she peered out of the kitchen window hoping to see Grace's torch. There was nothing to see apart from the rain lashing down and the trees being blown back and forth in the gale. The wind had truly picked up since she had arrived, and she was relieved not to be outside. Lou grew more and more worried for Grace as the minutes ticked by, she should be back by now, where was she? Suddenly Lou caught a glimpse of a figure standing in the middle of the garden, unfortunately the window was too wet to see through properly. She immediately swung the door open and scanned the tall grass,

"GRACIE!? Is that you?"

Lou gave a small scream as someone grabbed her by the left arm.

"Lou!? What are you doing? Quickly get back inside, you're getting all wet again!" Grace shouted through the storm and guided her friend back inside.

"I thought you only went to the cellar?" Lou declared, pulling the towel around her shoulders once more.

"I did. Sorry it took a while. I thought I knew where the box was and then I was so confused. I was lost would you believe it. I was just going around and around in circles."

"Well then…who was outside in the garden just now?" Lou asked, glancing once more outside.

"I didn't see anyone. Who would unnecessarily be outside in this weather?" Grace asked in a confused manner.

Lou agreed nodding her head and then gave a broad smile, "Nathan?"

Grace laughed with Lou and headed back into the warm room.

*

The month May was a much calmer month, the storms had passed and on this day in particular it was a fortunately warm day. Grace was bustling about her room trying on various dresses, wondering if they matched her heels properly and the ribbon in her hair. She finally decided on an off-white mid length dress, white goes with everything, she told herself and made for the front door.

"You off Grace?" Her mother asked, hobbling over from the living room on a stick.

"Yes Mama. I've left you and Pa some cold meat and sliced bread for supper, and there's some iced barley water in the fridge too." Grace replied and bent down to kiss her mother's cheek. She was almost out of the door when the phone shrilly rang.

"Can you get that please Grace? I'm not quick enough these days."

Grace picked up the receiver, "Hello? Grace Forrester."

"Gracie!" Came a voice which sounded relieved, "So glad I caught you. I have a major problem!"

"Hello Lou. What's your major problem?" Grace answered, grinning to herself as everything to Lou was a major disaster.

"We have no wine, only the lemonade Ian's mother gave us. Matt has just dropped off some warm beer which is cooling off in an ice bucket. You're the only one I know who has a wine cellar with actual wine it! So can you Gracie…please?"

"I'll see if I can find something," Grace answered, there was a tap and a slam of the front door, "I've got to go. See you later Lou."

She hanged up the receiver and made her way to the hallway and was surprised to see a man standing there, "Nathan!"

"Hello Grace," He responded and held out some pink carnations with gypsophila, "For you."

Grace blushed slightly, "Why, thank you Nathan. I'll put these in water."

She made her way over to the kitchen and reached up for a small vase and said, "You are lucky father has taken a tablet to help him sleep, he is completely conked out. By the way you look smart."

"I've been invited to Lou and Ian's engagement party. Ian gave me a personal invite."

Grace was stunned in confusion, she was under the impression that Lou and Ian weren't all that keen on Nathan, she murmured, "Oh, ok."

"Grace, I'm just going up for a lie down," Grace's mother muttered and headed upstairs.

"Ok Mama," Grace called after her, and turned to Nathan, "Since you're coming, maybe you can help carry the wine."

"Wine?"

"From the cellar."

Nathan nodded, pretending to understand and followed her out of the back door and round to the left side of the house. There were two loose boards on the floor and a padlock sitting neatly in the middle, keeping the boards locked tight together. Grace unlocked the padlock and threw it to one side, before pulling up one of the boards by the handle. She flicked on a torch and headed down the steps, cobwebs and dust clung tightly to the ceiling and various shelving towers. The wine racks were positioned neatly in a row at the back of the cellar,

Grace made her way over and pulled out various wines, some she put back and others she placed in a crate. Nathan grew bored and wondered around the dark hole, feeling his way along the shelves and stubbed his toe on a large object in the process. He couldn't see what it was, so he brought it over to the steps to get a better look.

"Hey Grace. What's this chest?"

"Don't know Nathan. I hardly come down here. It probably belongs to mum or dad when they first moved in years ago." Grace replied, continuing to examine bottles.

Nathan pulled at the lock so rusted with age it came off easily in his hand. He slowly pushed up the lid, which opened stiffly with a groan. There were various bits and pieces in the box, it looked like a memory box.

"Look Grace. It's a picture of your mother when she was young." Nathan exclaimed, pulling out a black and white photo.

Grace walked over and shone a torch on the picture, "That's not my mother."

"Look, there's a bracelet. You should have it Grace, it suits you."

"No thank you. It doesn't belong to me."

Nathan pulled out a jewellery box with some long brown locks of hair in it, he placed it down in disgust and picked up the next item, "Look I found a poem!

<u>An Ode to She</u>
An ode, a tale
To the girl so pale
Her eyes were green
Her face was lean
Woe betides a banshee's wail

A dress of white
She wore that night
The day the banshee's wail
Came to claim her body frail
Vanquishing her soul of light

Her body lay
To be found next day
Torn on the rocks below
Nothing to cure our sorrow
May our wrath pay

To your kin and children
And generations of grandchildren
To your house and land
To your work at hand
Cursed be your life, forever, amen.

"Doesn't sound like a happy poem. Rather gruesome in a way." Grace said, taking the paper from him and folding it back up, "We should put these things back. It doesn't belong to us, it probably belonged to the previous owners."

She picked up her crate of wine and slowly and carefully made her way up the creaky wooden steps. Nathan watched her leave before quickly pocketing the gold bracelet hoping to get it evaluated at the pawnbrokers. And after a second, he decided to pocket the photo too, maybe someone would know who the girl was.

"Hurry up Nathan! We're going to be late for the party and everyone is relying on me for the wine!" Grace called down the steps, picking up the padlock and turning it in her hand.

"Coming!" Nathan replied and stood back up. He was almost by the exit when a scuffle sound was heard behind him and a quick short sound of something being dragged. Nathan blinked but couldn't see into the dark properly and he rapidly darted outside, stumbling as the brightness of the light caused temporary blindness.

Grace clicked the lock into place and loaded the small handheld wooden wagon with the crate and together they headed downhill to the village.

Chapter 9
Present Day

"More tea?" Ann asked, holding the teapot above my cup.

I accepted as she poured in more lukewarm charred coloured tea.

"I assume you have more questions to ask? Isn't that what usually brings a policeman to your house?" Nigel asked amused, stirring in three heaps of sugar and a large quantity of milk into his tea.

I felt my cheeks burn knowing I had been found out, "Yes, I have more questions, but I won't ask formally, just as a friend if that's ok?"

"Of course. Much better to discuss this case as friends."

I thanked him and fired the first question at Ann, "What can you tell me about your father? I've heard so much about him, but I still don't feel like I know him personally."

"He was called Colin Marsh as you're probably fully aware like. He was a wonderful father, used to buy us gifts, took us on donkey rides at St Heliers sands, fish and chips for afters. As a husband though looking back like, he was an awful man to my poor mother who suffered. In the end it was just me, mum and my sister Emily, mother only just managed to fix a job in cleaning services and that sort of thing."

"Did you or your mother know about the affairs?"

"Oh yes. I was about eight or nine years I reckon. He had such a full-on job it never occurred to me he was going to houses and not working at all. If you understand me? As for mother, she always knew. Like, she wasn't stupid."

"What was his job?" I asked curiously.

"A painter and decorator, who worked long hours and always overtime late into the night. You can see how strange that sounds!"

I agreed as the rest of my soggy biscuit fell into my tea, "How did he meet Grace?"

"I don't know, I was only a little girl then. Like, he probably saw her in the pub or village, and he was a great talker and very attractive. Most girls swooned when he walked into a room!"

"Bet the husbands and boyfriends didn't like that!"

"No, they did not! Most of the fights that started around here were all his doing. It was all a game to him like."

Nigel placed his empty cup down with a clatter, "Did you tell Tom about Gladys?"

"Gladys?" I asked, my face frowning in confusion.

"Mmm," Nigel continued, "You probably know that Ann's mother refused to let him home after his arrest and eventual release? Well, he moved in with a young girl who had only just left school. They had two children together, I reckon Gladys was pregnant at the time of his arrest and was hoping that Colin would divorce his wife and marry her. Even after a few years had passed and Colin had filed for divorce on the grounds of separation, he still didn't marry Gladys."

"Not a man who was good at keeping his wedding vows though," I stated, "He shouldn't have married in the first place!"

"No, he should not. But it's not for me to say, I'm just the local vicar. I give advice whatever the situation is and try to avoid giving out a stern talking too."

I turned to Ann and asked, "Do you think…that your father murdered Elsie and John Forrester?"

"No!" Ann almost shouted and then in a calmer voice, "No, he did not. I'm not saying that because he was my father like. He was a proper bully who didn't care tuppence about anyone, he got into a lot of scraps, but nobody was killed were they? And he also had loads of girlfriends who left him, and he just moved on to the next one, didn't feel a need to get his revenge so to speak! Why would he kill Grace's parents? There was no point in it at all! Like, if he was upset, he would take it out on Grace, not her parents."

"So, you're saying your father wasn't a killer?"

"That's exactly what I'm saying."

There was a pause in the room, Ann left to make some coffee, which gave me time to change the subject,

"What do you know about a boy who died in the same place as Jenny?"

"Up on the cliffs you mean? I don't remember…how long ago was it?" Nigel asked, reclining back in his chair and placing one leg on top of the other.

"I'm not sure. Apparently, you found him?"

Again, there was another pause whilst Nigel thought to himself and waded through the memory bank in his head. Ann returned and placed the filter coffee in the middle of the coffee table and pushed the top down. As she was pouring out hot steamy beverages Nigel suddenly exclaimed,

"Daniel! Daniel Gates."

"Daniel Gates?" Ann asked with much confusion in her voice, "That man from the estate agents? Like, the one who died up on the cliffs?"

"Yes dear, that's the one."

"Who's Daniel Gates?" I inquired, declining a fourth biscuit.

"He used to work in the village at the estate agents…when we had one that is!" Nigel explained and told the story, "A very young man, not quite thirty if I remember right. It was I think ten or eleven years ago now. I found him the next morning very close to where Jenny was found, he was lying at the bottom of the cliffs not moving. At the time I couldn't see who it was from that distance, only later Ann told me, word got round the village pretty quick!"

"Was it also an accident or something else?"

"An accident, I'm sure. He was up there at night, and I remember now very well it was a foggy night, we had fog horns on that night. Very rarely that happens unless the weather is so severe. Last time we had fog horns on was two years ago, fortunately no one died that day."

I was shocked at how similar the cases sounded, "Jenny Hops and Daniel Gates both died in the same place on a foggy night, bit of a strange coincidence?"

Ann agreed with me, "Yes, it is. Like, I noticed that too."

Nigel laughed out loud, "Best not go up there on a foggy night then! It's obviously a very dangerous place to be, and if you're stupid enough to go up there on a foggy night…well what can I say? Look, coincidences happen all the time, no need to make a mountain out of a mole hill!"

I knew it was best not to argue with a vicar, so we finished our drinks in almost complete silence. Nigel brought up the latest sport and wondered how much up to date I was with the football and cricket. Since my arrival sports was the last thing on my mind, England was playing against Scotland tonight though, I couldn't afford to miss it!

*

Later that afternoon the wind picked up once more and pierced through my warm coat sending my body into shivers. I rubbed my arms and jogged slowly on the spot hoping to warm my body up as I waited for Lydia to finish her shift. Linda was the first to leave the premises,

"Evening Tom! Can't stop, voluntary work at the town hall, it's bingo tonight. Supper is at 7pm. Bye!"

I smiled to myself, did Linda ever stop? She still amazed me how she found the time to do so much, no doubt there would be another excellent supper on the table and on time! I glanced through the window and caught a glimpse of Lydia in the backroom, after a second the light turned off and she walked over to the door. She reached for the rest of the lights, stepped outside and pressed a button on her key fob, and we waited for a moment for the shutters to come down.

"Michael won't be long. He said he'll be down just after five." Lydia explained and sat down promptly on a bench looking rather worn out. Sure enough a Land Rover appeared from around the corner and stopped right next to them. A tall man with a flat cap on his head and still in his country tweeds jumped out of the car and opened the passenger side,

"Evening sister. Let me give you a hand."

Michael helped his sister clamber into the large vehicle and looked at me and said, "You're in the back with the dog. Hope you don't mind?"

Elvis was at this point breathing heavily on the window and having recognised me, slobbered the glass with a long pink tongue. I opened the back door and immediately Elvis started barking and tried to jump on me with delight. I pushed him back and sat down, clipping myself in whilst Elvis tried to sit on my lap. Michael was obviously taking some delight from his dog being a pest, every now and again he smirked at me in the front mirror. He also deliberately drove slowly, 'have to be careful of the potholes' was his excuse. What a liar! As if a Land Rover was bothered about a few potholes, they were built for rough terrain! Eventually Michael pulled into his drive and helped Lydia out and together they walked towards the farmhouse.

"Take Elvis round the back, will you?" Michael called out and closed the front door firmly.

At this point I was fuming but I needed to control my temper if I was to find out anything from this irritating man. I slammed the car door unnecessarily loudly and took Elvis by the collar and headed down the side of the house. Lydia was already waiting for me by the back door and let me into the kitchen, leaving the sorry looking dog in the conservatory.

"Sorry about Michael. He has no manners. Hardly surprising he has ended up alone." Lydia explained and gave me a wet flannel to wipe my sticky slobbered face. "What will you have to drink?"

After serving out some of the wine that Lydia found from the previous night, we made our way to the front room where Michael was already lolling on the sofa in front of the fire.

"So, P.C. plod is back. More questions is it sir? At least you asked to come this time and brought my sister for protection." The man raised his chin up and gave a raspy laugh and then wiped the supposed tears from his eyes, "Go on then. Fire away. I'm listening."

"I saw Lydia in the café the other day and she's told me a lot of interesting things." I began sitting on the rocking chair.

"Like what?" Michael asked, giving his sister a cold stare.

I told him what me and Lydia had discussed about their father being a possible suspect. And whether there was anything in it about a cursed box at The Larches. There was a quiet moment in the room where Michael collected himself and sat up right and pondered.

"Well…" Michael started, "The box is an old bedtime story, about curiosity and nosing into other people's possessions and how nothing good will come of it, it's just a fable. Mum would tell us that story every time one of us went through another's belongings, hoping we would learn from that tale."

"And the photo?" I questioned.

"It's in the attic along with the rest of the unwanted household junk. It's mostly old stuff that belonged to my parents. The wife took everything with her, left nothing behind."

"I know where it is, it's not in the attic," Lydia piped up and deftly left the room.

"LYDIA!" Michael roared and went after her, knocking his whiskey on the floor. I pursued after them leaping up the stairs two at a time and raced along the corridor. Michael was already wrestling the picture out of her hand, quickly I stepped in the gulf between them and snatched the picture for myself. Fortunately, the frame was still intact, and the glass hadn't broken. Michael subsided and holding his head low, ambled quietly back downstairs.

"What was that about? Has he gone mad!?" I asked, placing an arm around Lydia's trembling shoulders.

"Yes Tom, he has gone mad. It's the photo. He's obsessed with it, just like dad was."

"What's so…" I began and suddenly I saw. It was a black and white print, faded slightly yellow and the edges curled brown. Yet those eyes were mossy green I could swear to it and her hair was a dark shade of brown, her lips were full and sweet. Her long flowing dress of the palest blue dotted with tiny flowers and laced at the edges. There was an unearthly glow around her, I could see her in my vision next to me, I could smell roses, I could feel that long hair wrap around my body and lift me. I didn't know or understand what I felt, all I knew was, was that I was deeply in love with the girl.

"Where is she?" I quietly asked, my eyes transfixed on the picture.

"I don't know. She's probably died now judging by the age of the print." Lydia responded, taking the picture gently from my fingers and placing the girl back on the window ledge. "Let's go back down. Michael has hopefully calmed down by now."

I didn't want to leave that photo behind, but I obediently followed Lydia back down the stairs, my heart was feeling heavier with each step. Michael was looking sombre and stared deep into the flames of the fire, toying with a fresh glass of whiskey on the rocks. I refilled Lydia's and my glass before resuming my position in the same chair.

"So, you saw her then?" Michael asked.

I nodded and took a much-needed sip as Michael continued,

"Beautiful, isn't she? I got rid of everything of mum and dads, but for some reason I couldn't get rid of the picture, I love her you see."

I did see as I too was falling in love with a girl long gone from this world, my heart skipped a beat every time I thought of her. I smiled coyly to myself as a vision of her appeared in my mind and I closed my eyes for a second to visualise her better.

"Probably why dad went off his rocker, he too was in love with the girl. He was in love with mum don't get me wrong, yet whereas this girl is a mysterious human being unknown to him, mum is a real human being in the flesh and someone whom he knows well. You can't build a life on a photo of someone you love, you need a real human for that, and mum was that human." Michael concluded and relieved himself of a deep sigh.

I looked over at Michael and noticed he was a bit drunk as he unsteadily raised a glass to his lips and narrowly missed. Lydia left the room to turn on the lights and feed the hungry pooch waiting next door.

"Lydia thinks dad did it." Said Michael.

"Did it?" I asked, forcing myself to focus on the present and not the past.

"Mum's parents. She thinks he killed them you see, he said something stupid. Now what was it?"

"He said, 'Did you see their bloody faces? There wasn't anything left.'" Lydia answered for her brother, sitting down next to him on the sofa.

"Doesn't mean he did it though? He probably was passing by, sensed something wasn't right, went upstairs and saw them." I reassured Lydia who was looking very anxious and run down.

"I reckon it was mum who killed her parents." Michael stated, downing the rest of his glass.

"Michael!" Lydia exclaimed.

"Oh what! Did you know Tom our grandparents were invalids towards the end? Grandma had several strokes which made her eventually bed bound. Grandad had cancer and could barely get around. And poor mum running around them all day and all night, willing to give up her teaching career and almost turned down dad's proposal. It wouldn't surprise me in the slightest if she finally lost it and decided to kill them. And mum with her soft heart was probably wanting to put them out of their miseries instead of letting them sit there and wait painfully for death."

"Oh Michael, how could you say that about our own mother?"

"You're the one suspecting our dad! He says one thing stupid and immediately you assume he's the killer! He has a horrible temper and throws things, but I've never known him to pull out a gun and threaten someone! Remember the bailiffs after mum died? Wanting money which you Lydia finally paid for. Dad didn't threaten to kill them or throw anything at them, he just shouted and swore his mouth off and slammed the door in their faces! Does that sound like a murderer to you?"

Lydia's eyes welled with tears, and she numbly nodded and agreed with Michael, "No it doesn't. But he's no more a murderer than our mother."

I listened intrigued to this sibling argument gaining more information about this couple, such a shame Grace wasn't alive to give her own testimony. Nathan was my only chance for more information, unfortunately he was a bit crazy and just as arrogant as his son.

"It's getting late." Lydia finally said and stood up and wandered to the living room door. "Linda said your supper will be ready by 7pm."

As I was getting my shoes back on, I was shocked when Michael said, "I'll give you a lift back."

I hesitated wondering to myself if it was safe being with a drunk driver, although Linda's house was only a few minutes by car down the road. I had a feeling Michael wanted to say something else to me, so I thanked him and after saying goodbye to Lydia I hopped into the front seat. But I was wrong, Michael didn't have anything to say to me at all, that is until we parked outside The Pines.

"I apologise for my rude behaviour," Michael began and pressed his forehead against the steering wheel, "It's all too much."

"What is?" I asked, undoing my seatbelt.

"Mum and dad. Mum wasn't the angel and sweet child as everyone makes out, she had a dark side. She could lash out verbally and left my dad with a few marks upon his face, self-defence she told people. I've always blamed her for the murders, but dad is equally as capable. I've never told anyone this, when I was a boy…well…teenager really. My parents were arguing and screaming at each other, nothing new there really. Only this time, I heard my dad crying and apologising and saying, 'I'm sorry, it was an accident', over and over again. I thought he was just apologising for being a prick to my mother and hurting her in some way. And then he said something like, 'I didn't want too, it was all for you Grace.' I didn't want to believe it was dad. I didn't want to believe it could be either of them."

"What is it you think your father was talking about?"

"The murder of my grandparents. What else?"

Yes, what else? I thought to myself, although clearly it was all coincidental and he could easily have been talking about something completely different. Michael had obviously leapt to only one answer, when there could be other avenues to explore. I needed to talk to Nathan again if I was ever to find out the answer. I clambered out of the vehicle and raised a hand in farewell as Michael sped off back to the farm. Noticing I was ten minutes late I briskly sped to the front door which was conveniently left unlocked.

"Sorry I'm late." I called out, removing my outdoor clothing and hanging it on a peg.

"Linda's out. Didn't she say? She's got bingo duties at the town hall. Close the door will you? Fish and chips are in the oven keeping warm, hurry up though, the footie has just started!" Arthur replied, his eyes transfixed on the screen. I grabbed my supper and a can of lager and joined him on the recliner sofa, pulling the lever next to me and levitated my legs.

Chapter 10

Later that night I woke up with a start. I checked my phone, and it was past two in the morning. I glanced around the room and wondered what had woken me up. The full moon shone through the crack in the curtains, illuminating the corners and casting dark shadows on the walls. I crept over to the window and peered out, the garden gate was shut this time, and no one was lurking. Tired from a long day, I climbed back into bed and pulled the duvet high over my head and was almost asleep when suddenly I heard. The gate was creaking back and forth, deftly I jumped to the window and looked out, there wasn't anyone around. The back door clicked open, and a torch light shone on the path, as Arthur Storm strode over to the gate and shut it with a firm bang. Linda called out something about padlocking the gate at night, next thing I heard was the pair walking up the stairs and retiring to bed. Following morning the Storms were preparing breakfast, the smell of bacon wafted up the stairs.

"Morning Tom. Sleep well?" Linda asked, placing a plate of full English under my nose and a large cup of filter coffee. "You look awfully tired, don't tell me it's the sheets or the bedding for that matter. We had a new mattress put in last year and the blankets aren't that old, only a few years, I picked the best you see from the St Louisham housewares. Oh, is it that the room is too warm for you? I know winter is on the way that's why I put the heating up so soon, maybe too soon, judging from the black shadows under your eyes. How about we move you into a different room, with a …"

"Linda! You talk too much!" Arthur interrupted and stuffed more eggs into his mouth, "Let the poor boy eat his breakfast, a bit of food will do him good."

"Yes. Right, I'll go and check on the croissants. As Arthur wisely said, nothing like a bit of food to put colour on your cheeks."

She abruptly left the room looking slightly put out as she busied herself with the next course of breakfast.

"Women. Talk too much, I don't want to appear rude, but Linda can talk all day unless you butt in."

"It's ok. Too much talk is better than no talk." I said, cutting my salty bacon in pieces and scooping crisp sausages onto a fork.

"Spoken like a true policeman!"

"Arthur, I can't help but feel like I'm having déjà vu. I've woken up each night at the same time and your garden gate has been open and swinging. Is that normal?"

Arthur tugged at his collar, "Yes well. Me and Linda are going to get a padlock on it soon, so don't worry yourself. I'll get one today and hopefully tonight you can have a better sleep."

Linda waltzed in once more carrying a tray with croissants and pots of jam and honey, by this time I was feeling rather full, but I couldn't say no to a pastry! After breakfast with no further plans I retired to my room and decided to go through my notes once more:

Notes:

1. *Jenny Hops, died from cliff 20th of Sep. ~~Possible suspect, Sean Conway~~. Accidental.*
2. *~~Young boy~~ Daniel Gates died same way years ago. 10 years ago. Approx. Need to ask Ann or Nigel for facts. Done.*
3. *House 'The Larches' derelict for years, couple who owned it Mr and Mrs F. Shot in the face or head. John and Elsie Forrester.*
4. *Grace, daughter of Mr and Mrs F. Dead now. Husband? Nathan Barnes, retirement home. Her son Michael Barnes lives at the farm. Daughter Lydia works at the café.*
5. *Ann's father Colin Marsh deceased - arrested and released in connection with Mr and Mrs F's death. Moved in with Gladys.*
6. *Other suspects of murder of the Forrester's include Grace and Nathan Barnes.*
7. *Roger Hope knows more than he is letting on.*

I leaned back against the bed's head rest, my mind was going around and around in circles. I came here to find out about the girl Jenny and put the matter to rest for the parent's sake. And instead, I've found myself knee deep in a double homicide from sixty-four years ago, with only a few suspects and no witnesses. That was the problem, I had no witnesses. Who could I ask that was alive and old enough to remember the situation for what it was? Nigel and Ann were children at the time, they had no idea what was going on, only the presence of police everywhere. Nathan was in his twenties then, although he wasn't going to go down that avenue and reveal what he knew or what he saw that day. Roger probably knew more than he was letting on, but it was like drawing blood from a stone with him. I grinned broadly to myself and realised how stupid I've been, Brian practically told me from day one!

*

"Well look who it isn't. I knew you'd come home one day. What'll it be guv? Half Badgers or pint of Guiness?"

I thanked Brian and settled for a half pint of Badgers Ale. The barman pulled out a stool for me and sat opposite, polishing a glass with a tea-towel which looked similar to the same one from when I first arrived.

"What brings you back then?" Brian asked, picking up another wet glass to dry and polish, "Looking for more suspects? I heard you weren't satisfied with Colin Marsh, even though he clearly did it."

"I've been told he's a ruffian and a rogue, but murder? I don't know, he sounds so shallow, too shallow to commit a double murder. Anyway, it's not suspects I want, it's witnesses."

Brian let out a low whistle, "Good luck with that! Most folk from that era are either dead or deranged in an old people's home."

"I was actually going to ask about your parents. Didn't you say that they were friends with Grace?" I asked and helped myself to a bowl of nibbles.

"Yes, that's right. Deranged those two. Off their rocker most of the time, you'll find them at home. They won't hear of going into an oldies home. Alice pops over every morning, checks their pulse when they oversleep and keeps house. Here, I'll give you the address." Brian whipped out some paper from under the counter, patted his body for a pen, and scribbled down some strange looking words, "Here. They live right by the sea front, just head out of the pub and keep going in a straight line. Big yellow house, red windows and a small bonsai looking thing in the front garden and pebbles arranged in a funny circle. It's what dad calls a Japanese garden. Oh, and it has a tiny pagoda."

"Thank you. I'll head over now." I said, and zipped my coat back up, ready for the bracing cold and damp drizzle.

"I'll give them a tinkle, let them know you're on the way. Old people love it when you call. See you Tom."

We shook hands and I headed in the direction of the Fletcher's residence. The sea wall was soaked through as wave after wave crashed over the side. The boats of the harbour that spent most of the time in thick sand were now bobbing up and down fiercely on the water. A couple of men were at the other end of the harbour sharing a long pole between them and winding the gears of the harbour gate. It was all very dramatic and fascinating to watch, the storm clouds grew darker, and the rain got heavier. I dashed along the sea front and down a path which held only a few houses, Brian was right, the house was extremely obvious and stood out easily. I raised the dragon knocker and knocked on the red door, there was a long pause and I wondered if they heard me. Brian did say he would call ahead, the rain suddenly turned into a downpour, hurriedly I knocked again and this time a young girl opened the door,

"Yes? Oh, you're drenched! Come in quickly!"

I squelched into the hallway and removed my soaked coat and hat, shoes and socks, there was nothing I could do for my trousers. The girl pressed a towel onto me and dried my hair with a smaller towel she held,

"There." She said and smiled a warm smile, "Bit better. Tom, is it? Brian just phoned."

"And you're Alice, right?"

She smiled that smile again which radiated her bright blue eyes, "We know each other already it seems! Come through I'll make some tea."

I followed her into the kitchen and watched her petite body reach up for the teapot and place four teabags into the pot. She brushed her short blond hair from her face as she daintily turned to fill the kettle at the sink. It took a while for the water to boil but I wasn't in a hurry, it was warm and comfortable in the kitchen with Alice. She would make a great wife, I thought to myself, oh get a grip Tom, you don't even know her! With the morning tea complete I once more ambled behind Alice into the living room, pictures of African scenes lined all the walls and marble elephants were carefully arranged on the mantlepiece. I admired the painted portrait of cheetahs which hung above the fireplace, two cheeky little cubs chewed lovingly on their mother's ear.

"It's a good painting, isn't it? Had it commissioned when I was in Africa twenty years ago now." Came a shaky voice from behind me.

I turned to face an elderly looking man, very round in the middle and no waist to show, he looked a bit like a snowman in the flesh. He held out a wobbly hand,

"Ian Fletcher, my wife will be along. She's in her little shed, enjoys working in peace and quiet. Apparently, I'm too noisy for her." He chuckled and promptly sat down and turned the television on, horse racing blared out of the screen, "Alice is too good for us. Would you like some tea?"

Alice waved her hand through the living room door, well wrapped up for the outdoor extremes, fortunately the rain had died down now. She was just heading off. I was sorry to see her go, hopefully there would be a chance that I would bump into her when I was around in the village. Ian put an end to that idea though,

"Alice lives in St Louisham. Comes over every day in her little Mini just to check on us and makes sure we're topped with provisions. Godsend that girl, little angel."

The back door slammed shut followed by the sound of feet stamping on a mat. I assumed it was Ian's wife as Ian poured out another cup of tea and placed a fairy cake on a plate with some biscuits.

"Hello, you must be Tom. Lovely to see you. I was working in my shed, got a bit distracted." She directly spoke, eyeing me up and taking in my features as I stood there looking at her. "And turn that television down Ian, I can hear it from the bottom of the garden!"

Ian introduced his wife, "Tom, this is Lou."

"Lovely to meet you Lou," I said and waited for her to sit before sitting down again, "What work is it that you do?"

"Sewing mostly, I make clothes for dolls, have done for sixty-five years now. Now you haven't come for a lesson on dolls clothes, have you? Our son Brian knows everything in this village, so naturally we know everything about you." She explained, her eyes twinkling as dimples appeared in her fine cheek bones.

I warmed to Lou straight away, for a lady her age she was in remarkable health, must be the sea air. How old would she have been in 1958 I wondered? Grace was in her early twenties then so Lou might have been the same age. Which would mean she would be in her mid-eighties by now!

Lou must have read my mind for she said, "Me and Gracie were at school together when we were children. Best friends until the day she died, that was a sorry day for all of us. Poor girl, she's had such a beastly life, first her parents and then Nathan who was an absolute beast to her, we never liked him did we Ian?"

Ian gave a grunt, not paying much attention to our discussion.

Lou continued, "And then her son Jacob getting crushed at the farm. Lydia and Michael with their divorces. Sophie has done extremely well though, never married sadly and died alone with cancer."

"What can you tell me about Grace and Nathan? I only have Michael and Lydia's say on it, Michael is extremely angry about everything and blames both parents for the murders, Lydia is too scared and upset and thinks her dad might have a say in it. I was hoping you could tell me something about Grace, how well did you know her? And Nathan, was he really as violent as people make out?"

"Gosh. That is going back quite a bit. Me and Ian weren't even married when it happened, it was a month before we wed if I remember correctly. Yes, that was very strange."

"What was?"

"Well shortly after the deaths of Gracie's parents, Nathan was in an absolute rush to get married, didn't even propose or ask Gracie. He just booked the Church as soon as he could. Gracie only found out he booked the Church a week before the wedding was to take place. It was due to take place the week after our wedding, so we sadly had to cut short our honeymoon so we could be there for Gracie."

"Despicable." Ian grunted and looked up at Lou, "To force Grace's hand so soon after her parent's death.

Her parents weren't even buried yet when the wedding took place."

"Why the rush?" I asked, shuffling closer to Lou so I could hear her better.

"He didn't want Gracie to be alone, he wanted to give her a proper home to live in and didn't want to go about it in an unchristian way. That's the excuse he gave, even though Gracie had an aunty who was more than willing to open up her home to her." Lou explained, placing her cup on the table.

"Was Nathan a violent man would you say?"

"Yes and no. He wasn't violent when we first knew him, arrogant and irritating, a law breaker and no manners. He became violent after the deaths of Gracie's parents, and he got worse over time. Several times we've gone over to her house to calm her down and help with the children."

"And Grace?"

"Violent? No! She had a secret temper that only Nathan could bring out of her. Made her verbally abusive. Verbally and not physically."

"And what do you know about the house? Lydia mentioned a strange box, and when I was at Michael's yesterday there was a photo of a girl which apparently came from the box."

Lou shook her head and appeared dumbstruck for a moment, "I don't know anything. Sorry."

Ian answered for her, "She doesn't know anything about the box or the girl. The house though is another matter, it's not right somehow."

"Not right?" I curiously questioned.

"Mmm," Ian continued and coughed, "Strange happenings up there. Always has been ever since we used to go and see Grace. Unusual noises and well strange. They had builders. Do you remember Lou? Scared out of their wits, left the place only half finished. What scared them? That's your real mystery."

Yes, I thought to myself, The Larches, the same story kept popping up again and again from people that had visited that place. I had to go back there, curiously I asked,

"What was the name of the builder in charge?"

Ian hummed to himself for a minute, "Baker. Something Baker. Me and Lou used to joke about the man being in the wrong profession! Saying that, his granddaughter Florence is a baker in St Heliers and then she married."

"You'll find his son Mark is still living in the village, he has carried on the building trade, hopefully his own son will continue in his footsteps." Lou added.

There was a slight pause whilst I thought about what to ask next.

"Where you there at the house at the time of the murders?"

"No. Unfortunately." Lou replied, picking up her crochet and pink wool.

"What happened that day? If you don't mind me asking." I inquired.

"Not much to tell. I got a phone call from Gracie, saying that she had come home to find her parents…well…shot. She phoned from Roger and Diana's house. Diana was consoling her when I arrived at their house. Roger had already rung the police. Nathan turned up later wanting to take Gracie home to his place, I put my foot down and took Gracie home with me instead."

"Do you have any idea who did it?

"Most of the village thinks it was Colin Marsh." Ian chuckled, spilling tea on his lap, "That man liked his women and starting a good punch up at The Red Lobster. He was an arse, not a murderer, but a complete arse!"

"So, you don't think it was him?"

"No. But I tell you who I think it was. Nathan Barnes. His behaviour afterwards was mighty shifty and in the years that followed his behaviour only got worse. Guilt I reckon, it was eating him up from the inside."

"Apparently he was there at the time of the crime." I boldly stated, wondering if it would have an effect on this couple.

"Was he?" Lou exclaimed, sitting up right, "Well that is news to me! Why didn't he say anything?"

"Guilt," Ian announced abruptly, "That's why he didn't say anything Lou. It was guilt."

Guilt, I thought to myself, it explained why Nathan was so hesitant to talk to me. But was he guilty? Unless he confessed himself, I knew there would be no way to be sure. I needed to speak again to Roger. Why didn't he mention he was the one who called the police? Roger obviously knew a lot about this case, he'll be giving a confession next!

Chapter 11
1958

"Grace! GRACE! Will you get those men to stop banging! It's giving me a horrific headache and I can't sleep!" John Forrester bellowed, pressing a pillow against his ears which did little to dim the noise.

Grace pretended she couldn't hear him and blatantly ignored him and continued to serve out cups of tea and biscuits to the builders. It had been three months since the surveyors had been to check over the house and give their final report. Most of the window frames were eroding away from the brickwork, a large crack in the living room ceiling was very disturbing. Rotting floorboards was mostly likely the answer, but they wouldn't know until the top floor had been ripped up. Rusty pipes in the kitchen with a constant leak under the taps and slow drainage problems. The roof was sagging, and small holes were appearing where tiles failed to exist. And to top it off, the chimney had half broken off in the recent thunderstorm, bricks were still piled up in the fireplace and soot lay on the hearth rug. Grace's mother had spent the last few weeks mending, pressing and ironing clothes for the villagers in a bid to raise enough money to fix the house. Grace had been giving out private teaching lessons as well as baking cakes and small treats to sell and had extended her business to the next town. Between the pair they had only just made enough money to pay the builders and for the cost of supplies.

Tony Baker turned up on the nineth day of July as arranged with his small band of men, and after introductions made a tour of the place. He read the surveyor's report, tutting at the damage and using a hammer tapped at the walls and ceilings.

"It's going to be pricey Mrs Forrester," he said and gave a short whistle, "But I'll do what I can to keep costs low."

"Thank you, Tony. You're very kind." Elsie Forrester replied and waited for him to unload his tools before standing aside whilst he made his way to the kitchen.

"Scaffolding is arranged for tomorrow. The lorry will turn up shortly after with supplies and other bric-a-brac. Not much I can do today. I'll take a look at your pipes though whilst I'm here."

"Thank you, Tony," Mrs Forrester repeated and sat down with a flop on the sofa.

Tony looked at her with fondness and sympathy, what it must feel like to be old, in a house falling about your ears and trying to make ends meet.

And that is where Grace found herself a week later, providing for the builders as well as keeping her father in check. She was reaching the end of her tether as she watched two of the men yanking up the floorboards with a crowbar and shining a light on the boards below.

"Mmm," one of them tutted, "Rotten right through. How much I wonder?"

He pulled up more floorboards and pushed the little desk away from the wall.

"We need the boss on this one," said the other. Both of them stood up and left the room leaving a mess behind for Grace to step over as she approached her father.

"Afternoon Papa," she said and sat at the end of the bed, "Egg and cress sandwiches, your favourite. And a small cup of coffee, just don't tell the doctor. He'll be here later to check on you."

John was surprisingly humble as he received his lunch and ate with satisfaction, "Are those home wreckers nearly done yet? The noise they make will be enough to wake the dead! How can an ill man sleep with so much noise?"

"Sorry Papa, it's only been a week. Tony said it'll be another two months at most, it's a big job."

"Two months? Do you want me dead?"

Grace sighed and patted her father's knee fondly and proceeded back downstairs and into the main hub of the rubble. Tony was lifting large crates of bricks down from the lorry, his strong naked arms glistening with beads of sweat in the summer heat. Spotting Grace coming downstairs he called out,

"Grace, do you have a minute?"

Grace glanced over at him and felt a hot rush through her body and her cheeks flaming bright red. She hurriedly fanned herself hoping that Tony would assume it was just the heat and said, "Of course, would you like some iced lemonade?"

"Sounds good, yes please."

Grace busied herself with the drinks and headed out of the back door and unfolded two metal chairs for herself and Tony to sit down on.

Tony gratefully received the cold drink, "Mmm. Much better! You're probably wondering how far we've got? The kitchen pipes and drainage are fixed, you've probably noticed the water is running smoother now. Unfortunately, the structure of the house is nowhere near finished, we haven't even properly started. Look, I don't want to beat about the bush, and I'll come straight to the point. It's not safe to live here if we're to do our job properly. You and your family will have to move out if you want the house fixed."

Grace continued to stare towards the bright blue sea which was peppered with tiny silver sequins. A gust of wind blew her hair about her face, she quietly asked, "Where are we going to live? Father has cancer and mother is so tired."

"I don't know Grace. Unfortunately, I can't help, I'm just telling you as it is."

Grace silently nodded and a worried expression passed over her face as she stood up to head inside, "I'll just let mother know."

*

After several phone calls to a variety of friends and neighbours asking for help and immediate accommodation, they finally found someone who could help. Jeff and Susan Jackson willingly opened up their home at Morecombe Farm, Susan already knew Grace and was fond of her. She didn't have any children of her own and felt sorry for Grace and took Grace under her wing as her own daughter. Susan deliberately placed Grace in the room next to her and her husband's, whilst Grace's own parents shared the room opposite, next door to the bathroom. It was a lark persuading John to move from his bed to the farm, he was a stubborn man and refused to walk further than the bathroom or downstairs for a midnight snack. At first, he was in denial and pretended he didn't know the Jackson's, and then when he did realise who they were he pretended that Jeff Jackson was nothing but a wild bushman from the outback. Which wasn't strictly true, even though the Jackson's were originally from Australia. It wasn't until the doctor turned up after being told what the situation was and a few checks later revealing that Grace's father was in perfect shape to move to another house, he finally obliged. The doctor persuaded John into his car and drove him over to Morecombe Farm and settled him down in his new room. It was quite an ordeal, but Grace was relieved when her parents were finally settled and comfortable in a stable home and for the first time in months, she slept the whole night through.

The next morning Grace woke surprisingly early to a pink dawn and birds breaking out in song, the sun had yet to make an appearance which meant it must be about five. Jeff was already up, and Grace watched him leave via the front gate and down towards the barns where the cows were. She opened her window to let in the farm noises and the smell from the cattle waft in, she smiled for she adored a farm and would give anything to live on one. She duly went back to sleep again and was awakened by a sharp whistling noise at about seven, Grace peered out of the window and immediately cowered down under the windowsill. Nathan Barnes, the one person whom she did not want knowing that she was staying there, even though it was near impossible to hide forever. After breakfast and finding her parents still out for the count, she decided to head back home and see if the builders had turned up yet.

She was surprised to see the scaffolding had already gone up and the tiles had been removed from the roof. What was left of the chimney was still there, not for long though as someone drove a sledgehammer through the remaining blocks and carefully removed the last few bricks that were still clinging.

"What do you think? Pretty impressive?" Came a voice from behind her.

She turned and smiled shyly, "Very. How did you get the scaffolding up so fast?"

"We like to start early, gets the job done quicker." Tony replied, appraising her in her casual yellow summer frock. "Well got to get back on the job, several planks need replacing."

Grace nodded and watched him as he strode past with large strides and marched up a ladder two rungs at a time. When he reached the top one of the other builders hoisted up a thick heavy plank towards him which Tony easily grabbed and threw onto the pile.

Then without warning a heated conversation was heard from inside and grew louder as two men reached the front door.

"Tony!" One man yelled, Grace immediately recognised him from yesterday as the lad who was doing up the floorboards, the man shouted again, "Tony!"

"What is it, Ern?" Tony replied and slid down the ladder with a thump at the bottom.

"I quit! That's what up!"

"Quit? You've only been here two days. What's the rush?"

"I can't work with you lot, always taking my things when my back is turned, skulking in the rooms thinking I can't hear you. Guess where I found all my nails Tony? In Graham's toolbox."

"I've already told you Ern! It wasn't me!" Another man retaliated, "Why would I take your nails when I've got my own?"

"I don't know Graham. What I do know is that I'm leaving! You can finish the job yourself."

Ern marched off towards his little car parked at the end, slammed the door and drove off with such speed he left a dust trail.

"Well…" Tony began and scratched his head, "That was over dramatic, we can still manage with one less man. Come on boys back to work!"

The other men that had gathered round to listen to the drama picked up their pieces and headed back to whatever it was that they were doing. By lunchtime Grace provided the men with lunch and lemonade, heeding Tony's warning not to walk through the house in case of flying debris from the roof. She laid the sandwiches and crisps outside on the little garden table and fetched more chairs from the cellar. Just as she was unfolding the last chair she heard Tony shouting for her,

"Grace! GRACE!"

Grace deftly ran around the house to the front garden. Tony was still at the top of the scaffolding sweating profusely even after removing his shirt and tying it around his waist.

Grace couldn't help but admire his fine physique and toned muscles, but now wasn't the time to humour an angry man, she called sweetly, "What is it, Tony?"

"Didn't I say earlier that you can't go inside just in case something heavy falls on you?"

"I only went into the kitchen, sorry Tony. I thought you all wanted something to eat and drink."

"Why did you go upstairs? You could have got hurt!" He fumed and climbed down the rungs.

"What?" Grace asked in a confused way and stuttered, "I didn't Tony. Honest, I only went into the kitchen."

Tony eyed her and watched her already red face grow even redder, "I saw you, Grace. Don't lie to me!"

"I'm not! Your lunch is on the table. I'm going back to the farm!" Grace retaliated and stormed off down the path and up the road, her eyes misted with tears. She was so upset she didn't look where she was going and bumped straight into Nathan.

"Nathan! I'm so sorry! I wasn't paying attention and I wasn't looking where I was going…"

"It's ok Grace," Nathan soothed and held her close, brushing his face into her hair, "What's got you so upset?"

Grace told him of her argument with Tony and how he disbelieved her, "He accused me of lying. I'm not a liar Nathan."

"It's ok, I believe you. Whatever he saw, he saw wrong. I was coming to find you actually. Your mother is asking after you and I said I'll look for you and bring you back."

"Thank you, Nathan. That's really sweet of you." Said Grace and wiped a loose tear from her cheek and allowed Nathan to place an arm around her waist and guide her home to the farm.

*

The month of July passed by pretty fast to Grace's surprise, she had been so busy with her teaching lessons, looking after her parents and helping on the farm she only just realised it would be August next week! Nathan had invited her to the first barn dance of the year which she accepted with a graceful blush as she found herself warming to him. Susan and Jeff were decorating the barn and getting it ready for the weekend, Grace and Nathan helped with the bunting and blowing up balloons.

The builders were halfway through their project, the support beams between the levels were replaced and the pipes were also replaced. There were still some floorboards left on the side to nail back into place. The window frames still needed fixing or replacing, depending on how bad it was! The roof now proudly held new beams with underlay and Tony had started placing the tiles back on, some new some old to save on cost.

Ern had humbly returned to the work force admitting that he needed the work, Tony happily accepted him back and left him with the replastering in the kitchen. Graham kept his distance to avoid another accusation being fired at him, even though he was completely innocent.

"Grace?" Ern called out, quickly looking behind him as he felt her presence.

"Grace? I didn't see her arrive." Tony responded and splattered more plaster on the wall.

"She was right behind me."

"Not likely Ern. She would say hello or something. Grace is too polite to hide around the corner!"

The two men continued to work in almost complete silence, Tony hummed a tune from a song he heard that morning. Without warning Ern leapt up from where he was crouching, sending the tray of plaster flying across the room.

"Ern!" Tony retaliated and said sternly, "What is wrong with you?"

"Something touched my neck!" Ern replied crossly scratching the nape of his head.

"Probably a spider! Go outside and cool off, I'll finish in here."

Ern obediently left the kitchen and huffed to himself as he searched his body for spiders or insects of any sort. Tony chuckled to himself and continued to work, picking up his tune as he went along. A very quick puff of warm air breathed onto his neck, Tony jumped up angrily,

"Ern? ERN!"

Ern was outside having a smoke at the end of the garden kicking up grass with his feet, he looked up as he heard his name called,

"What's up?"

Tony turned a grey shade of white and struggled to speak, "What…? But you. Who is inside?"

Ern shrugged his shoulders and threw the rest of his fag onto the floor and stamped on it thoroughly, "Don't know. Graham is up on the roof, been hammering non-stop since this morning. Carl is having the day off and Matt was fixing the floorboards, but I saw him stop for a lunch break just now."

Tony quickly ran to the front garden and the first thing he noticed was Graham and Matt sitting on top of the scaffolding sharing sandwiches and banter. Tony grabbed his hair and rubbed his head fiercely with his palms, what had just happened? There was only one conclusion, he ran back inside the house and cried out,

"Grace! Grace! Where are you hiding? Is this a joke? Are you upset? Answer me, Grace!"

The other men walked into the house and looked at each other and could only stare wide eyed as Tony made a scene of himself running around the house yelling.

Graham grabbed Tony by the arms and firmly lead him outside, "Tony! Get a grip mate, Grace isn't here. She's at the farm getting ready for the barn dance, nobody has seen her around here."

"I know she is here," Tony stammered, "There is someone in the house who is playing a prank and I don't like it."

"I'm heading inside now to help Matt fix the last of the floorboards, I think you should stay here and have a strong coffee."

Tony could only nod in agreement.

For a while there was order as Graham and Matt headed upstairs to the bedrooms carrying the rest of the planks between them. Loud hammering sounded out as nails were rammed home and planks of wood were slammed onto the floor. Graham swung round to grab the last few nails from his toolbox when he noticed they were missing. He searched the floor and patted his body down and scratched his head in bewilderment,

"Hey Matt, you've seen my nails? They've all gone."

"No." Matt called from the opposite room, "Have some of mine, I've got…"

"Got what?"

Matt took a long while to respond as he circled the room, "I've lost my nails too."

"What!?"

"That prankster is back. Why do I get the feeling they don't want the house fixed? We need to tell Tony about this."

Graham agreed with Matt and gathered the rest of their tools, a horrific crash sounded from the stairs, the house shook, and debris fell from the ceiling. Fearing something awful had happened to their friends the men ran towards the staircase and stood frozen to the core in terror. The planks of wood that were carefully piled on the landing had been thrown down the stairs in a careless fashion. Tony and Ern appeared at the bottom of the steps.

"What happened?" Tony asked, staring at the mess.

"That's it! I'm done! Our nails have mysteriously disappeared, and the planks of wood have got thrown, all by an invisible prankster or a madman. I've had enough!" Matt angrily explained, still shaking from recent events and strode over the wood and headed to the front door.

"Sorry Tony. I know how heavily you rely on me, but this is too much," said Graham, shaking Tony's hand and followed Matt out of the door.

"I'm too am sorry Tony," said Ern, laying down his pallets. "I can't fix a house with unexplainable happenings going on. I too quit…again!"

"Not you too Ern." Tony sighed and shook his head.

Ern could only nod as he silently left the house behind him. Tony watched subdued and worried, with a contract to fulfil and so much work left to be done. Yet he too knew something wasn't quite right, something was afoot about this house, something or somebody didn't want this house repaired.

*

Grace was speechless when she heard that Tony was calling it a day.

"Why?" She asked looking bewildered, "I don't understand."

"I'm sorry Grace. We've been experiencing a lot of unusual happenings that we can't explain. We've never come across anything like it in our building career. I finished the floorboards, and the tiles are back on the roof, I couldn't leave that unfinished. Unfortunately, the plastering, walls and windows are still in need of repair, but the worst is behind you now."

"Right. Well thank you Tony for all your hard work."

"I'll draft up the receipt for you. Again, I'm sorry Grace."

Grace waved him goodbye as she headed back inside, her mother was waiting for her by the door.

Elsie asked her daughter, "Can we go home now?"

"Yes Mama. We can."

Later that evening as Grace was packing the last of her clothing, she could hear her parents arguing from the room across the halfway.

"NO! I will not Elsie! I absolutely refuse. REFUSE! You hear me."

"John, we have to pay them for the work they've done already. Tony has been ever so good and charged us only for the work he has done and deducted the price quite severely."

"NO Elsie! If they wanted to get paid, they should have completed the work and done it properly. Not half finish it and then make some lame excuse about the house being haunted. How long have we been living there and not a squeak!"

"I can't explain it John, but we must pay them. It's not right if we don't."

"Well tell them to come back and then I'll pay them. Matter is closed!"

There was a silence as Elsie knew she was defeated, Grace listened to her father's heartless decision and decided that Tony and his employers will be paid one way or the other.

Chapter 12
Present Day

Another morning dawned, I had slept through the night peacefully without disturbance and was surprised to see it was nearly nine o'clock. The house was extremely silent, which probably meant that Arthur and Linda Storm had already left for work. I closed my eyes for a further fifteen minutes, my stomach grumbled, and I decided it was probably best to get up. Linda had kindly left me some cereal on the table along with a mug and some useful instructions:

Morning Tom!
I hope you slept well, Arthur told me he padlocked the gate, about time too.
Milk is in the fridge, it's a fresh bottle so no need to worry about it being gone off. Croissants are ready to go into the oven, 180oC for no more than 5 minutes, make sure the oven is hot first. Fruit is in the fruit bowl in the kitchen, I know how much you like apples so have as many as you want. See you tonight, supper is at 7pm.
Linda

I grinned to myself as I got the milk out of the fridge, Linda loved to fuss and took the role of mother hen rather seriously. She must think I am an incapable teenager and not a fully grown man who has lived on his own for the last ten years, I thought to myself. After scrapping the last of the jam off my plate with the cold croissant it was rather late in the morning.

There was someone I needed to talk too, and I reckoned they weren't an early bird, the first time I saw him he was still in his pyjamas!

After getting ready to go out, I realised that the garden gate was still padlocked and I had no key, the picket fence was too flimsy to jump over so I had no choice but to walk down by the road. Approaching the main gate on the road a Land Rover came blundering down the track at speed and skidded near the barrier engulfing me in a cloud of dust. I coughed and spluttered waving the sand and dirt from my face, a man hopped out of the car and swung the gate open with a crash.

"Morning P.C. plod. Gorgeous day. Good timing, you can lock the gate for me. Ciao!" Michael sneered and climbed back into the Rover and gave a cheeky wave as he revved his engine and zoomed through the open barrier, speeding down the street. I was not impressed even though I was getting used to Michael's wild ways, gently I closed the gate with a click and firmly pressed the lock into place. A while later I found myself outside the pastel blue house with the large number '1' on it once more. I firmly rapped on the front door, not expecting an answer and after a minute had passed, I thought it was best to leave when the front door suddenly swung open.

"Yes? Tom Jones, back again. Anything you want?"

I looked at Sean and was surprised to see him looking so much healthier, his black shadows had ceased to exist and the stubble around his chin was clean shaven. He was almost smiling if he hadn't been scowling at me.

I didn't invite myself in because I knew what the answer would be, so I said instead, "Hello Sean, you're looking well! I have a few questions to ask if that's ok. Only take five minutes."

Sean hesitated and then quietly nodded, "Only if you don't accuse me this time."

"The other night about two in the morning, were you anywhere near the houses on the cliff top?"

"You're asking if I went to that house? The answer is no, I've got no interest in that place."

"Are you sure?"

"Course I'm sure! I wouldn't say no otherwise, would I? Any other questions or are we done?"

"The bracelet, you said that Michael sold it to the pawnbrokers and then you bought it yourself."

"Yes, that's right."

"Are you sure it belonged to Michael's wife and not to his mother? Michael said that his wife took everything with her when she left so why would she leave her bracelet behind?"

"He probably found it and got rid of it soon as possible. Why else would he say it was his wife's?"

Sean asked, looking thoroughly bored talking about jewellery.

"Unless he thought that it belonged to the wife when actually it was his mother's the whole time." I pondered thoughtfully, stroking my chin.

"Whatever. You're the cop here. He said it belonged to the missus and it doesn't bother me who it belonged too. Can't think why you're so interested in a trinket anyway? If you don't mind, I have to go out soon."

I stepped back from the doorstep as Sean closed the door, locking and bolting it from the inside. I wondered what secrets this young man had to hide to have so many locks on the door. It was heading on to lunchtime, a good excuse to pop into the café and see Linda and Lydia.

*

Lunch was soon over, and the minute hand was getting frightfully close to my arranged appointment. I knew I was going to be late, so I put my best foot forward; climbing the coastal steps continuously found me in better shape than ever before. Soon I was ringing the doorbell of The Maples exactly on time, beating my previous record by two minutes. Again, the elderly lady opened the door,

"Hello Tom. Come in, Roger is in the study waiting. Whiskey or something less strong?" Diana welcomed and wandered through to the kitchen.

I followed through after her and accepted an ice-cold beer, she showed me to the study before returning to the television, the lunchtime news had just started.

"Well! Detective Inspector Jones. What brings you to my house this time?" Roger chuckled and shook my hand firmly.

I took the same seat as before and sat down, "I met the Barnes family."

"The alive ones or the dead?" Roger interrupted.

"Both."

"Aah! And how do you sum them up?"

"Well, the dead ones didn't say much," I joked, "The alive ones…I can't make them out. Nathan Barnes has clearly lost his mind. Michael is one of the worst human beings I've come across and Lydia is kind and helpful yet constantly living in fear and worry."

"Strange bunch, aren't they?"

"Lydia thinks her father had something to do with the killings, Michael thinks it was his mother until he confessed later his dad could have been equally guilty."

"Don't forget Colin Marsh. The villagers swear it was him and nobody else." Roger put in, leaning back to smoke a cigar.

"There are very insistent," I agreed and declined a smoke myself, "Why are they so convinced it was him?"

"His reputation you see, he didn't have a very good one, did he? Although I reckon it was more to do with the fact he upset and broke most of the girls in the village, the villagers just wanted their revenge and they wanted Colin to pay."

I wholeheartedly accepted Roger's way of looking at the situation involving Colin Marsh. It didn't look good for him, yet I felt something nagging at me telling me it wasn't him.

"What about Grace and Nathan Barnes? Could they be involved?" I inquired scratching my forehead.

Roger looked strange for a moment and shifted his shoulders uncomfortably, "Grace. So beautiful and so young and naïve. Why did she marry Nathan Barnes? It ruined her life, even though she was too stubborn to admit it, Nathan was no good for her. He was charming yes and was there when she needed someone. Unfortunately, he was a bully on the inside. He was a dictator, constantly adamant and extremely self-righteous, it was about him you see and no-one else mattered. Why did he marry Grace?"

I too shifted uncomfortably and rubbed my upper arms for it was something that was constantly on my mind, why did they marry each other? Why the rush on Nathan's part? Why didn't Grace leave him?

"One more thing," I began, clearing my throat and placed a hand over my fist, "I've been talking to Ian and Lou Fletcher yesterday. Apparently, Grace came to you straight after she found her parents and you were the one who called the police."

"Yes," Roger murmured quietly and stood up to look out of the window as he reflected on the past, "Was like yesterday."

"What happened?"

"Who knows really. Me and Diana were young newlyweds when we moved up here, only lived here about a year when it all happened. You see, I got offered a job on the farm tending to the sheep that the Jacksons had just bought from market. It was the beginning of August of 1958. A Sunday, we had just got back from Church and there was an urgent knocking on our door. I opened it and there was Grace covered in blood, screaming and crying, she was inconsolable. Diana soon saw to her and calmed her as best as she could, enough for Grace to blurt out that her parents had been killed. I instantly called the police and Diana later called for Grace's friends."

"Grace was covered in blood?" I almost shouted as this unexpected news hit me.

Roger solemnly nodded, "Unfortunately yes. The police had a lot to say about that, it really shook her up. Nathan was with her constantly and shouted down the police officers persuading them that she had nothing to do with it. I agree."

"But if she was covered in blood. Then surely she must have been guilty?"

"If you remember Detective Inspector, the shots were apparently fired from the doorway. It's not possible for blood to splatter that far, you probably saw the wall was covered and the floor was only partially covered. If she fired those shots she wouldn't be covered in blood." Roger explained gruesomely and flicked ash into the tray.

Naturally I didn't remember the shots being fired from the doorway for this was new news to me. I had already built up an image that the shots were fired close range for some reason, whoever did it must be an excellent shooter. Unfortunately, Roger was right about the wall being the only thing that was blood stained, how did she get blood on her clothes then?

"Why are you so sure that she is innocent?" I asked, closing my eyes as I felt a headache coming on.

"Truthfully, I've only known her for over a year before tragedy struck, but she was the sweetest thing I've ever known. I was a fair bit younger than her, me and Diana were teenagers when we married couldn't wait to marry and get away. Grace would come over with cakes and home-made bread, and when Diana was pregnant, Grace would regularly carry out shopping trips and help around the house whilst I was at work. She even assisted with the birth. In the short time that we knew her, she never once had a vile temper only a positive vibe that filled her and made her glow. She always went out of her way to help others, no job to big or small, you could always depend on her. When her parents died, she was so distraught, would a guilty person be so upset? I would expect crocodile tears from a murderer. But Grace, she was crying genuine tears. And that is why I'm so convinced on her innocence."

"Did you keep in touch with Grace after events took place?"

"Sadly no, not as much as me and Diana would like. She got married pretty swiftly to Nathan, moved to the village and then spent the rest of her life at the farmhouse. We hardly saw her and when we did, she had lost her glow and wore a shroud of darkness upon her shoulders."

"What did you think when Grace married Nathan only a few weeks later? Ian mentioned her parents weren't even buried yet."

"That's right," Roger confirmed, "Talk of the village. Most of us were planning the funeral and making arrangements, next thing we're told is, forget the funeral it's now a wedding! A very sombre wedding it was too, Grace was holding back tears, Nathan looked fierce. Only a few friends turned up, Lou and Ian had to cut their honeymoon short to attend, and an aunty of Grace's also showed up, we never saw her again."

"Why did they marry?" I found myself asking, repeating what Roger had just said earlier.

Roger shrugged his shoulders, "It wasn't for love that's for sure, I've never met two people less in love than those two."

"Yet they stayed married and raised a family."

"Yes, that's true. I expect Grace just accepted her fate for what it was and made the most of it. She was like that. She always made the best of a bad situation."

"One more question Roger, completely random. Did Grace ever mention a box she and Nathan had found? It had a photo in it which is still at Michael's house. Do you know anything about that?"

"Sorry to disappoint you, Tom. I have no idea what you're talking about."

I sighed and stood up to say goodbye just as Diana walked through with her little tea trolley.

"Oh, going already Tom?" Diana asked in surprise, "Will you stay just for a bit longer? Can't let you go out hungry."

That's what I loved most about visiting the people of Morecombe, the women assumed I was starved and needed feeding and the men pressed beers into my hand. If it wasn't for the murder case I was trying to solve, it would have been my best holiday yet!

Chapter 13

It was getting late in the afternoon and the sun was almost at its end, the sky was on the brink of lighting up on fire. I still had one more mission to complete for the day, so I thanked the Hopes profusely for giving me their time and food. Soon I set off down the road in the direction of the farmhouse for a brief ten minutes and stopped outside The Larches. It still looked exactly the same, only something was different, it was when I reached the back of the house, I noticed that someone had been and strimmed the grass. Who? I wondered to myself. I entered through the back door once more and pulled my torch out from my pocket where it had been sitting uncomfortably all day. Nothing had changed inside. I decided this time to make a thorough investigation if I was to find that box. Ian had mentioned the builders fixing up the place until they decided to leave for some reason, which might mean that the box could have been lost in the rubble. I had no idea when Grace and Nathan had found the box, before or after the men had been.

It was growing darker inside as sunset was definitely imminent, I felt extremely wary and uncomfortable with the thought that someone could be watching.

Someone who had the ability to apparently scare off tough builders. The sooner I talked to Mark the better, perhaps his father Tony might have told him something about the house. I shone the torch into the living room, there was only furniture sitting along the walls and a short glance told me that there was very slim chance of anything being hidden. I wasn't entirely sure what I was looking for apart from the object being a box. Was it small? Big? Square? Rectangle? Was it made of solid long-lasting wood, or flimsy cardboard that by now must have disintegrated? The dining room also contained furniture and no hiding places anywhere. I made my way next to the kitchen, there were lots of cupboard doors and drawers. Steadily I opened each one in turn. Finding nothing I started closing them one by one. Reaching for the last cupboard door; it must have been a trick from the light of the torch. As I almost closed it, I could swear someone was standing in the living room. Nearly dropping my light on the floor in fright I quickly and fiercely grabbed the torch end, furious and scared at being so close without a light source. I shone the torch round rapidly and didn't see anyone. There was no box in the kitchen, I gathered myself and ascended upstairs. My heart accelerated as I climbed the stairs once again, hoping and praying that there would be no more loud unexplained noises.

There was no noise. There was nothing unexplained. There was nothing at all. Short of prying up all the floorboards in a hope that the box might be underneath, I was left stumped, the box clearly wasn't here anymore. It was now dark outside as well as in, the house was eerily quiet and uncannier than ever. I hated it, the feeling of dread and the feeling of being watched. I felt like a trespasser with the guilty feeling of a schoolboy searching the cupboards for a forbidden midnight feast. This house clearly still belonged to the previous owner and always had done. I left the building and exited round the side of the house. Unable to see where I was stepping my foot got caught in something and I fell abruptly onto my stomach scratching my face in the process. I grabbed the torch which had rolled away and guided the light towards my feet, I had fallen over a rung which was screwed to the floor. Strange place to put a rung, I thought to myself. I grabbed the rung and tried to pull it towards me but to no avail. I stood up properly and scrambled through the grass, pulling up roots and dirt violently. A minute later I noticed that the rung was part of a pair and a broken lock lay next to the rungs. A secret entrance? Or a shelter in case of a fierce storm perhaps? With so much dirt piled on I thought it was best to leave it for now and return another day with a shovel. Feeling disappointed I made my cue. This particular mystery will just have to wait.

The lights were fully on at The Pines, stuffing my dirty hand into my sleeve I rang the doorbell.

"Tom! I haven't seen you since lunchtime!" Linda exclaimed and kissed me fully on the cheek with a loud smack, "I saw you had a good breakfast, don't forget to wash up next time though will you dear? Ahh! You're all muddy! Take off your shoes please and that muddy coat, I'll pop it into the wash. What happened to your face? Did you walk through some brambles? Now come with me straight upstairs and I'll run you a bath and find you a flannel to dab your face. Lavender or camomile bubbles? I prefer the lavender myself, but Arthur insists on camomile!"

I immediately did as I was told enjoying the feeling of being mothered and dutifully followed Linda to the bathroom. It was a lovely hot bath and I immediately felt relaxed amongst the smell of camomile. When I had finished and dressed I made my way back down and approached the dinner table, Linda had plenty more questions to ask me,

"Did you find out anything today? Tell me you know who has done it. Any more suspects? You know, I've been thinking it over and I reckon it was Grace and Nathan Barnes who did it together. That's why he has such a hold over her. But what if Grace did it and Nathan saw, and he threatened to tell the police unless she did exactly as he said. Or Nathan did it and Grace saw him and…no that wouldn't work. Or how about Nathan did it and Grace found out only after they got married and by then it was too late and who would believe her? Nathan would only turn around and say it was Grace who did it! Why didn't she leave him if she knew, why did she stay? Did she know? Did she…"

"For goodness sake woman!" Arthur loudly exclaimed and thumped his fist on the table, "It's all very well to have your superstitions but none of it could be true! Why would Grace kill her parents? Why would Nathan kill Grace's parents? That's the real question here."

"Oh, right. You're quite right Arthur. Yes…it's the why that is puzzling. Why would they?"

"So, any more suspects Tom?" Arthur asked, tossing some roast potatoes onto my plate.

"Not as such. Apart from what you know already, Colin Marsh and Nathan Barnes. Grace Barnes has been mentioned a few times as a possible suspect but there has also been a lot of doubt surrounding that idea." I replied and helped myself to steaming veg.

"Knew it!" Linda declared with a broad beam of her face and her eyes lit up, "Didn't I say Arthur. It was Grace and Nathan Barnes who did it, or at least one of them! Not sure where that leaves Colin Marsh though? Unless…he is involved as well! Of course! It's a love triangle between them it all makes sense now, the three of them killed Grace's parents! Three people and two murders!"

Linda held her hands to her face and gasped, "What if there is a third murder we don't know about, what if each individual killed a person?"

"Linda you are rambling on a lot of nonsense and poking the hornets' nest so to speak. And you're forgetting once more. Why? Why did they kill Grace's parents?" Arthur sighed and poured more gravy over his supper.

I swallowed the beef I was chewing before asking, "Do you know Mark Baker? His father was the builder at The Larches, he was doing up the place when Grace was living there."

"His father was, was he? Didn't do a very good job of it!"

"Apparently, he was scared off. I was hoping to speak to Mark and see if his father told him anything."

"Mark is always busy I can give you an address for his office and his home address. He lives here in Morecombe, but the office is in St Louisham, I'll give you a lift in the morning."

"Thanks Arthur I appreciate that."

"Is Mark a suspect as well?" Linda asked returning with more potatoes.

I looked up surprised for I hadn't even realised she had left the room, I answered, "No he's not, I don't think he was even born then."

"Oh yes, silly me. Is it his father you suspect? Do you think Grace was having an affair with him? I got it! Grace's parents upset him in some way, so he decided to get his own back! Get his revenge so to speak."

"Don't be stupid woman!" Arthur demanded and muttered casually to me, "Change the subject please Tom!"

*

Mark Baker's office was situated in a little cul-de-sac off the high street with a few flats above him. His company was intriguingly labelled 'Bakers Builders' which must have left a few people scratching their heads in bewilderment. There was no pictures or description of what 'Bakers Builders' actually was or what they did! I pushed the door open and walked into a large almost empty room, a small white desk was in front of me, and a few plastic chairs lined up in a row by the wall. I hovered by the desk debating what to do next, nobody was around and there was no way of indicating my arrival. I called out but no one answered, feeling rather put out I left, shutting the squeaky door firmly behind me. As I turned, I noticed a short stout man of about thirty who had just climbed out of his car, he wore only shorts and a shirt which was extremely surprising for such a cold autumn day. I waited a while and sure enough, the man walked right up to me eyeing me up and down suspiciously.

"What's this?" He asked and then chuckled, "Loitering or are you waiting to come inside?"

"I've already been inside but no one was in." I explained standing back to let the man go in front of me.

"But we're not open yet," he began and turned the handle and muttered under his breath, "Not again!"

I was feeling rather confused by this point, however I followed him inside and sat on a chair and waited whilst the man walked through a door into what I assumed was the backroom. Immediately an argument broke out between him and someone else, I didn't want to appear to be eavesdropping and yet I couldn't help but listen in.

"I told you millions of times, you can let yourself in early, but you must lock the door behind you. We don't open till 9.30! A man is waiting outside, God knows how long he has been here!"

"I'm sorry Mr Baker. I didn't hear anyone…I swear!"

"No, you didn't! You had your stupid earphones in! Did you finish up the paperwork from last night?"

"No. I didn't have time, I already told you Mr Baker it was my girlfriend's birthday yesterday."

"Then make time! You could have done it first thing this morning!"

Their voices dimmed and the rustling of paperwork was heard.

"You're an incompetent idiot! The paperwork is an absolute disgrace and what do you mean you summed up the price wrong?"

"I don't know, I only wrote down what you gave me."

"That was for the last customer! She had her windows done. Now this customer had new drains and drainpipes put in. Isn't it obvious!? You know what…get out. Just go! You're fired!"

There were a few more heated words and a chair scrapped across the floor and fell with a crash onto the hard floor. The door slammed open unnecessarily loudly and a young boy stormed out, his face was fierce and red as a tomato. He looked at me and said,

"Stay away from that man. He is a cowboy builder, takes your money and leaves you screwed."

He stormed out of the front door and would have slammed it too if it hadn't been for the stiff hinges. I could only stare after him bewildered. Clearly, I had chosen the wrong day to speak to Mark. There was silence in the office for a few minutes, eventually the builder emerged from the backroom,

"Sorry about that, I had to tidy up a bit. I hired that young twat only a few months ago, he just left school and needed the work. Looks like I'll need a new secretary."

"I'm Tom Jones. I was hoping we could talk?" I extended my hand out.

"I'm sorry where are my manners," the man replied and shook my hand. "Julian Baker. Come through and I'll make some coffee."

I followed after Julian into a somewhat chaotic little office, this was clearly where the main hub took place. The chair was still lying on the floor, I picked it up and sat down and my eyes swept the room, taking in the many filing cabinets and paper strewn all over the worktops. A computer was tucked into the corner and a printer was positioned awkwardly underneath the table, making it impossible for anyone to position their legs comfortably. Julian was busy in the other corner of the room with his coffee machine, soon he passed me a frothy cappuccino and pushed some paperwork aside so I could rest my cup on the tabletop.

"You can press whatever button you like but it will always be a frothy coffee," he stated and sat down next to me. "So, what did you want to talk about?"

"I was hoping to talk to Mark actually, no disrespect. Is he in today?" I asked and sipped some of the froth.

"Mark? He doesn't venture this way much. I've taken over as manager, so dad just goes where he is sent and does the job. And I am left with the paperwork and disgruntled customers." Julian sighed and stirred some sugar into his cup. "I much prefer to be building you see and I'm still waiting like a fish on a hook for a suitable secretary. So far, no luck. Unless you're applying?"

"I've already got a profession." I began.

"Don't tell me! You're a bank manager? Or a manager of sorts in retail? You have that sincere look about you. You only get that look when you've reached the top."

"Detective Inspector actually."

"Detective Inspector? Right, well what brings you here?"

I explained briefly as I could what brought me to this part of the world and the investigation I was solving. Julian nodded all the way through not saying a word.

"So, my grandad was Grace's builder? He never said, unless I just wasn't paying attention, he did ramble a lot."

"Did?" I asked curiously in confusion, picking up on the past tense.

"Mmm. Died almost eight years ago, natural causes and a good age, he was nearly ninety!"

"That is a good age," I agreed and stared into the distance as I figured out the numbers, "So he would have been around thirty at the time?"

"I suppose so. I can't tell you anything I'm afraid. Dad can tell you more than I can, unfortunately he is out on a job at the moment."

"When will he be finished?"

"Don't know, not till late that's for sure. Look, if you're that keen on talking to my father I'll give you the address where he is working."

Julian rustled through some paper and pulled out a pink slip, "25 Mulberry Gardens. It's the other side of St Louisham, go through the town, first road to the right after the library. There's a for sale sign outside the house."

I finished my coffee thanking Julian and made my way to the other end of town, fortunately I already passed the library before, so I knew where I was heading. The house was extremely easy to find, scaffolding was built up the whole side of the house and a large sign hung into the road. There was another sign, please don't walk under the scaffolding, and an arrow pointing to the left saying, pedestrians. I noticed that the house was getting a serious facelift, plastering and painting were being applied to the front of the house and the sides as I made my way through to the back garden. A man with white hair to match his white overalls, blended against the fresh coat of white paint he was applying to the house. From a distance it must look like the can of paint he was holding must be floating in mid-air by itself!

"Excuse me! What are you doing back here? This is private property! Now I must ask you to leave." Called out a large burly man who grabbed me around the shoulders with one arm, half pushing and half leading me towards the front gate.

"Wait! Wait!" I cried out and resisted the large man, "I'm a police officer and I need to speak to Mark."

The big man stopped in his tracks, "Need to talk to Mark, eh? What about?"

"His father. Tony Baker."

"Well, that's different. Usually, the police want us to move our skips and building stuff off the road. He's around the back."

He turned around and walked back in the same direction that we had just come from and climbed up the scaffolding with ease. I looked up at the men conversing, clearly Mark struggled with his hearing, every now and again he placed a hand behind his ear and leaned towards the big man. The big man eventually jumped down and landed next to me with a thump,

"He's on the way down. Old geezer will probably take a while though." He chuckled meanly and strode off back to whatever it was he was doing.

He was right though, it took about five minutes till Mark reached the bottom of the last rung of the ladder, seeing me waiting he gave a smile.

"You wanted me?" Mark asked and led me towards a bench in the garden. "Something to do with my father Sam said. What about him do you want to know?"

"The double homicide of 1958." I began, and for the second time that day I retold my story.

"Yes, my father was the builder, you're quite right. He was redoing the Forrester's house. I was only a little boy of three years when it happened. I can't tell you much else."

"Didn't your father mention anything? Anything that can help at all?" I found myself almost pleading, a feeling in my gut telling me that there must be more.

"He was redoing the house that Grace and her parents lived in, the same year that they died," Mark repeated, "There is only one odd thing that I can tell you. My mother mentioned it to me once. When father was working at the house, he stopped halfway through. His workers just packed up and left, claiming that the house wasn't empty, and someone was still living there. Someone no longer a part of this world. An unwelcome resident so to speak."

"I've heard stories like that already," I murmured as I was familiar with this side of the story, as a memory from last night of someone standing near to me flashed into my mind, "So the story is true then? About the builders leaving?"

"Of course it's true!" Mark retaliated crossly and hastily changed the subject, "Did you know that Mr and Mrs Forrester didn't pay my father one dime for all his hard work?"

"What?" I exclaimed in shock, "He didn't get paid?"

"Not one dime. Mrs Forrester and Grace had raised the money between them. Mr Forrester however, he wanted the work completed before my father ever saw a penny of that money."

"How much did they owe him?"

"£410 and 8s. Today's money that would be nearly £15,000."

"Fifteen grand! And he didn't see any of it? Didn't he try and sue them?"

"They died shortly after. Grace married Nathan and moved into the village. My father was fond of Grace, he had the hots for her really bad. Even though he was happily married with two boys it didn't change the way he thought about her. He couldn't drag the girl he loved through the courts or ask her for the money after her parents had been so brutally murdered. Even though it plagued his mind for the rest of his life. Fifteen grand is a lot of money to miss out on."

I nodded in agreement, "What did Tony's wife have to say on the matter?"

"My mother? She never knew. My father only told me when I first took up the building trade, 'don't let anyone swindle you my son', that's what he told me, and he made me promise to keep it to myself. I have never forgotten it either."

We sat in silence admiring the mural on the wall opposite of pink flamingos fishing for shrimp in a baby blue lagoon.

"I'm heading home for lunch. Do you need a ride?" Mark stated, gingerly standing up and feeling his bones creak.

"Thank you. I appreciate a lift." I replied and left with him under the watchful eye of Mark's foreman. The van was parked at an odd angle on the kerb, Mark swept the passenger seat clear of paperwork and tools. After spending several minutes looking for the car keys, we finally set off.

"Is your mother still alive?" I suddenly asked, holding onto the door as we swung around a sharp corner.

"No. She died a few years ago." Mark answered, grinding the gears and slamming the van through a rut.

"Is there anyone alive that knew Tony Baker well from those days?"

"Only Nathan Barnes. Grace's husband. You'll find him in the retirement home. He knew dad well. He would come over sometimes and pay us a visit. That reminds me, Nathan and dad had a horrific argument one evening, this was sometime after the murders. I was ten years old then, I remember it well because it was my birthday."

"What was the argument about?"

"Don't know. Money problems, I think. I got given a new train from my parents, so my mind was elsewhere."

I sighed and leaned back just as we were approaching Morecombe. I hobbled out of the car with care as I could feel a bruise on my thigh. Mark sped off towards the Church narrowly missing a black cat that was lying comfortably in the middle of the road. This would be a good time to pop into The Pines, have some lunch and fetch a much-needed shovel.

Chapter 14
1958

Saturday morning dawned bright and beautiful with the promise of a splendid hot day and a pleasant warm evening. Grace was extremely excited, there was so much to prepare and still so much to do. After breakfast she raced over to the farmhouse and found that Jeff had already left for market with a few sheep and farmhouse goods. Susan had already started baking the many quiches and pies needed for that night, Grace placed an apron over her head and immediately set to work.

"Can't believe it's finally here. The first barn dance of the year!" Grace squealed excitedly, "I hope there will be lots of dancing and music and everyone I know will be there. Well…hopefully not everyone."

Susan gave a small smile as she accidently wiped more flour over her face, "Yes, Colin won't make an appearance, Jeff made sure of that. Unfortunately,

Nathan will be there, but I think you're starting to like him a little."

Grace splatted her dough onto the table and began to knead. "Not really. It's true I am seeing a nicer side to him, but he is still the rudest person I have ever met. So obnoxious!"

By lunch time the savoury pastries and sweet desserts and cake were finished and ready for the evening, Susan carefully balanced them on top of each other in the fridge. Jeff had arrived home earlier than expected having no success at the farmers market, some of his eggs got broken in transit and were therefore unsellable. After lunch several hay bales needed moving and arranging into makeshift tables and chairs, Grace tucked table covers around the haybales that represented the tables. By evening Jeff attached the last of the lights to the electrics and switched it on, the little lights lit up the barn inside and out like fireflies. It was dazzling and breath taking to see the reflection from the lights on the many coloured balloons and streamers. Grace ran home in her excitement and hurriedly dressed for the occasion. Her mother helped arrange her hair.

"Have a good time. Won't you love," said Grace's mother fondly as she tucked in the last hair pin.

"I will Mama," Grace replied and kissed her mother on the cheek. A noise was heard from next door, Grace popped her head around the corner, "Yes Papa?"

"I said, don't let those boys get too close to you. You know how boys are with their busy hands."

Grace smiled, "Don't worry Papa, it won't happen."

Elsie gazed lovingly at her daughter, remembering the time when she was young and about to meet John for the first time. He was so different back then, she sighed to herself. John had once been so charming and caring, always putting her needs above the rest and everyone liked him. It was only when they moved into their house, he became sour and bitter with uncontrollable outbursts of verbal rage and general hate towards other lesser people. She gave Grace a small wave as she watched her daughter leave the house and head back towards the farm at a gentler pace this time.

By the time Grace returned the night was almost about to begin, the band had turned up and were practising their country folk music. More people were arriving through the red barn doors, and she immediately took her place and offered out the drinks. The barbecues were lit and the aromatic smells of smoky and slightly charred meats and veg soon filled the air. There was a lot of merriment going around, and as the band got going properly, many couples took to the floor for the first barn dance of the year. Grace watched, laughing and clapping hoping that some man might swoop her off her feet at any moment. She glanced round and soon realised that a lot of men had brought their women with them, or the single men were watching other girls. After a bit Grace felt bored and sat down with a cold cider wondering when pudding would be served.

"Do you want to dance with me?" came a voice from behind her.

Grace recognised the voice and moodily huffed till her cheeks blew out, "Hello Nathan. No thank you, I'm enjoying my drink."

"Come on." Nathan begged, "I've been watching you all evening, standing there bored out of your mind, dying for a dance with a man who will swoop you off your feet."

"No thank you."

"Well, no one else is going to ask you," he responded rudely, "Look, everyone has a partner but you. I'm the only single man left so you have no choice."

Grace looked around the room filled with people dancing in their pairs, she closed her eyes and grimaced knowing that Nathan was right, "Fine."

He took her hand and led her to the floor and held her uncomfortable close to his body, fortunately it was a song she was familiar with, which couldn't be said for Nathan. Every so often he stood on her foot or turned in the wrong direction and at one point bumped into the couple behind. The song finally finished, and Grace was thrilled to be released from Nathan's grasp, Nathan however was reluctant to let go of her and pulled her into the next song.

"Nathan," she whispered through her teeth, "I'm tired, I want to sit down."

"Come on darling, just one more song. You love dancing." Nathan replied and swung her round the wrong way.

"No Nathan. I've had enough, let me go please."

Nathan's grip on her wrist only tightened more, Grace struggled to pull away knowing that she was causing a scene as a few people stopped to watch. A tall man had been watching her from the doorway and decided now was the time to be the hero of the moment.

"OI! She said back off!" Colin gave Nathan a push backwards causing him to instantly loosen his grip on Grace.

"Yeah!" Nathan retaliated angrily, "And what? Grace wanted to dance with me. It's got nothing to do with you!"

Several people had stopped to watch as the song came to an end, wondering what was going on.

"Grace doesn't want to dance anymore!" Colin growled, "You should respect her wishes if you want her to be with you."

"Respect? Respect?" Nathan scorned, "You show up here talking about respect? If you had any respect, go home to your wife! Stop flirting with Grace, she's my girlfriend, not yours!"

"You little swine, I'm going to kill you! I'm…"

Jeff Jackson had been watching the commotion from the doorway and quickly stepped in before the first punch could be swung, "Alright men that's enough! It's my party and I'm ordering you both to go home and cool it off. You're in enough trouble Colin, you weren't invited. So, I would head home if I was you before the police are called."

Nathan spat on the floor, narrowly missing Jeff's boots. Both men knew better than to get on the wrong side of Mr Jackson, they shoved their hands in their pockets and headed back to the village. Grace was thoroughly upset and made excuses to go home herself.

"Nonsense," said Jeff and hugged her in a fatherly fashion, "Now let me show you how a true gentleman dances with his partner."

Susan gave her husband a loving smile as she watched him pick Grace up and dance with her, if only they could adopt Grace and take her into their farm to live with them. It was nearly midnight by the time the dance drew to an end, Grace felt warm inside and extremely happy and sighed with content. The best party of the year by far, she thought, ok it wasn't a great start, but the end made up for it. Susan drove her home and waved from the car, Elsie was still awake and waiting in earnest for Grace to arrive home safe and asked,

"So, how did it go?"

*

Next morning was Sunday, Grace awoke and struggled to keep her eyes open, it was nearly nine in the morning. She could hear her mother downstairs in the kitchen bustling with some pans, her father was snoring contently in the next room.

"Morning Mama," said Grace as she walked into the kitchen and helped herself to a bread roll. "Mmm, bacon. What's the occasion?"

Grace's mother smiled, "Your father likes bacon rolls and he hasn't had one in such a long time. You know how it is with the doctor only allowing the healthiest of foods. Be a dear and take up his breakfast tray."

There was a huge crash from outside as one of the metal dustbins made a loud clatter, causing Grace to jump and spill the coffee all over her dad's breakfast.

"Whatever was that?" Elsie stammered, "Grace. Go and see what it was. I'll take your father's breakfast things."

Grace passed over the tray and cautiously headed outside turning her head in both directions anxious not to miss the culprit. She snuck around the corner and noticed the bin lid had fallen off the bin with a crash and landed next to the hedge. Grace sighed with relief. It was probably the neighbour's cat foraging for last night's chicken scraps. As she was about to head back inside, she heard a strange scuffling noise nearby, quietly she tiptoed in the direction of the noise. There was something in her cellar, every so often a scratching noise could be heard, she hovered by the cellar doors debating whether to open them or not.

"Morning Grace!" called a voice behind her causing to swing round crossly.

"Colin! You shouldn't sneak up on people!" Grace responded furiously.

"I didn't sneak, I was whistling as I was walking along, and I saw you and thought I'd come over and say hello."

"Hello Colin, and goodbye."

Colin laughed merrily, "Don't be like that Grace. Here. I've been shooting rabbits, would you like a pair?"

Grace smiled shyly, "Ok Colin. You know I can't say no to a few rabbits. That'll make a nice surprise for my parents, they're rather fond of rabbit stew."

Colin unslung a pair of rabbits from around his shoulders and passed it to her, "So what are you doing? I've been watching you hanging around like a burglar, lost your keys or something and trying to break in?"

Grace grinned, "No. Just investigating a loud noise which led me to a stranger noise in the cellar. You're braver than me and you've got a shotgun with you, do you want to find out what's in my cellar?"

Feeling like a knight in shining armour Colin gave a brave salute, "Of course! This takes a brave knight to investigate the rodents and other creepy crawlies."

"Just have a look please," Grace pleaded.

Colin nodded and slowly drew up the wooden boards, "It's dark. Have you got a torch Grace?"

Grace shook her head and was about to head back inside to retrieve one when a head popped up out of the cellar causing her to scream with all her might, "Nathan!"

"Nathan!" Colin repeated, "What the hell are you doing in there!?"

"I was tired and didn't want to walk home." Nathan explained with a yawn.

"What the hell is wrong with you!?" Grace exploded, her face reddened with fury, "You broke into my cellar for a sleep!? Who does that? There is something wrong with you! It's pitch dark in there and nothing to sleep on, how did you even manage to sleep?"

Nathan shrugged his shoulders in a pathetic manner, "I found it comfortable. I see you brought your boyfriend along."

Grace sensing a stand off quickly put in, "He's not my boyfriend, he just happened to be up here this morning."

"Oh. Just happened, did he?"

"Well at least he wasn't skulking around in dark cellars!"

Nathan sneered nastily as he realised, he had Grace on a hook and he could control her with his manipulative skills, "I wasn't skulking, I was sleeping. Colin is the one skulking, who actually shoots rabbits on a Sunday morning?"

Grace was lost for words, so Colin stepped in for her, "I like shooting rabbits. And as I was near the cottages, I thought I would pop in and see Grace."

"So, you thought you'd pop in and see if you could woo Grace with dead rabbits." Nathan laughed cruelly, "You're a joke Colin! No wonder girls dump you so fast! No wonder Grace…"

Nathan knew as soon as he said Grace's name that he had gone too far, Colin had lunged at him and knocked him sideways back into the cellar. Colin leapt in after him ignoring the shrouding darkness that enveloped them. Grace could only stand in horror by the doors peering into the blackness, listening to the fight that was going on and hearing the odd man cry out in pain. She ran back inside calling to her mother, fortunately her mother had heard the commotion and was already assisting John through the kitchen and out of the back door. Grace ran back towards the cellar, just in time to see Colin walking backwards up the steps with his arms raised in the air. Nathan wore a bloody forehead and a black eye as he aimed Colin's own shotgun at him, snarling with ferocious eyes as he stood there calculating his next move.

"Please Nathan," Grace cried, "Just put the gun down."

Nathan looked at her and blinked heavily, the black mist that was around him was slowly evaporating, he could almost see clearer now. Grace was standing at the top of the cellar and Colin was on the top step staring at him with fearful eyes as the barrel of the gun pointed to his chest.

Nathan felt a tear trickle down his one good eye and thought to himself, what am I doing? He dropped the gun, and it went off with an alarming bang, Grace found herself screaming again and flung herself on her mother who had just appeared. Colin fell to the ground and rolled back and forth holding onto his arm,

"You idiot! You almost killed me!"

Nathan just swayed on the spot unaware of what was going on or what was happening.

"Didn't I tell you Grace?" John spluttered, having just made an appearance on his wooden sticks, "Nathan is a bad man. There is something wrong with him, he is mentally ill. He could have killed someone today. It might have been you if it wasn't for that man over there."

Elsie was applying towels to Colin's flesh wound, "You should come inside, let me tend to your wounds."

Colin refused her generosity and gently pushed her away, "No, thank you. I've had enough. I'm going home. Sorry Grace, this wasn't what I had planned."

Grace silently nodded, crying uncontrollable tears. Colin deftly picked up his gun from where it had fallen, gave a nod to the family and ventured back homewards towards Morecombe.

John glared furiously at Nathan, "I think it was time you went home too. I told you I never want to see you again and I meant it. Next time you show your face I'll kill you myself."

"John!" Elsie exclaimed.

"I mean it Elsie! This man is seriously ill," John responded and turned to Nathan, "You should go get some help. And if you value your life, you will stay away from Grace, never go near my daughter ever again."

Nathan could only hang his head and kick his heels, unaware of what was happening to him. Solemnly he left the house and slowly ambled in the direction of the farmhouse. Elsie and John were thoroughly worn out from such an ordeal that Grace insisted they both had a lie down. After her parents were comfortable in bed with a fresh pot of tea, Grace donned on her best scarf and headed to Church arriving only five minutes late.

Chapter 15
Present Day

The Larches didn't carry off that sinister feeling by day, it looked like an ordinary house in dire need of repair. Arthur had joined me on the expedition as it was a half day for him. To be honest, I was very glad for company and not having to face the unknown alone this time. I showed him to the side of the house and the rungs that stuck out of the earth.

"Ah yes. We've got one of these too. It's the cellar, convenient in a violent storm as well as storing the wife's rubbish," Arthur heartily laughed and rammed a spade home, "Yes, the doors are under here, good solid wood this stuff, should have rotted eons ago!"

I wedged my spade underneath the soil and pushed and pulled as hard as I could but to no avail.

"No, no." Arthur tutted in a fatherly way, "You're better off cutting squares with the hacksaw I brought and then lifting the squares with a spade! Mind the wood though, don't want to cut all the way through."

The soil was firm, and the hacksaw easily cut through the roots of grass and weeds, curiously I asked Arthur something that had been on my mind a long time, "Arthur. Your gate, does it do that every night? Swing open by itself."

Arthur's face was bright red, through embarrassment or exertion I couldn't tell, "Only now and again, it's usual for this time of year. It's the wind you see, and the gate not being closed properly."

"After two in the morning each time?"

"Coincidences happen," Arthur chuckled nervously and wiped the sweat from his brow.

"Have you seen anyone lurking around the bottom of your garden at night?"

"Lurking? No. I've seen no-one. If you are thinking back to that Jenny case, I didn't see her that night. We didn't hear anything either. Me and Linda were in bed fast asleep."

Satisfied with my work I stood up and admired the doors which were now visible, "Finished, shall we open and see?"

The hinges were stiff and rusted with age and the doors were proving to be a struggle to open, together we pulled one of the doors and it finally burst ajar. Cloud and debris flew out as we pulled open the other door, we coughed and waved the dust away. For a while we couldn't see anything, me and Arthur pulled out our torches and shone it into the darkness. Shelving units lined the walls containing items that were unrecognisable under years of thick dust and cobwebs. The air was still musty and cloudy, it was a struggle to see through properly. I kept spluttering and placed my sleeve over my mouth as I was finding it hard to breath.

"Ooh. Some nice Bordeaux is sitting here," Arthur exclaimed pulling out a few bottles and purred, "Chateau LaFleur. Very nice, extremely expensive. How did they afford such wine? Chateau Certan, very swish! Do you think anyone would notice if I took some wine bottles?"

"Very unlikely, it's been sitting here for God knows how many years! Who would notice?" I replied, rolling my eyes at Arthur's intellectual knowledge of vintage wines.

"I'll just take them outside then, that will surprise Linda when she gets home!"

I could only shake my head in disagreement, Linda wouldn't know the difference between vintage wine or cheap wine from the garage. The air was clearing now, dust particles hovered in the atmosphere like fairy dust, twinkling in the light from the sun. Arthur came back promptly,

"There's blood on the steps. Did you see it when you came in?"

I shook my head for I hadn't noticed, "Blood?"

I made my way to the stairs and banged my foot against a large treasure chest sitting near to the steps. The lock was already off and rusting next to the box, I thought to myself, is this the mystery box? Carefully I opened it, inside was only a few trinkets. A small jewellery box lay open, I wondered if it could have once contained the gold bracelet Michael claimed to be his wife's. The only thing remaining was long strands of dark hair, possibly brown or black. An image of the girl from the photo flashed into my mind for she had hair just like that. A piece of paper was under the jewellery box, it was yellow and faded and it was a struggle to read. It was written like a limerick although the rhyming was faulty, an awful poem about the girl's demise. I knew how she died now yet I only wished to know her name and who she was.

"Amy." Came a voice behind me causing me jump up. I turned and noticed Arthur reading the poem over my shoulder.

"Arthur! You made me jump!" I responded crossly, closing the box firmly. "Who's Amy?"

"I'll tell you when we get back, it's getting late." Arthur replied solemnly and headed up the stairs. I followed suit, noticing the blood drops and carefully avoided them. The sun was setting once more, the sky was blood red underneath the black clouds, the atmosphere was silent and still. We were almost by the back gate when there was a cry in the distance, a morbid and terrified scream of fear. I gripped Arthur's arm and noticed he too was pale.

Arthur mumbled, "The banshee's cry. We need to go now Tom, this place. There is something dreadfully wrong with it."

"Grace and Michael were right, this place is cursed," I quietly added, and the men quickly made their way back as the sun completely disappeared from the sky.

After we had our supper of reheated spaghetti bolognese, we sat in front of the television with my now habitual can of lager.

"Are you going to tell me now. Who Amy was?" I demanded, tired and frustrated after a long day and having to wait a few hours longer to be told the tale.

"Yes Amy. I've got to warn you though Tom, it's only a local tale." Arthur grinned and clicked his can open.

"If it's local, how come I haven't heard of it?"

"Well to be honest, I got it out of Brian one evening in the pub. Some friends of his was celebrating and they were all properly wasted! I believe it was his grandmother or grandfather who told him the story."

"And? Who was she?"

"I tell you the way Brian told me," Arthur began dramatically and spoke in a deep tone, "It was twilight, and the sun was yet to disappear, and the stars were yet to make an appearance. A young sailor boy climbed into his fisherman's boat along with his father to have one last turn at catching fish. They were caught unawares in the fog which had slowly been creeping into the bay. The boat was smashed to pieces on the rocks and the bodies weren't to be found. The girl Amy was so distraught when she heard her lover to whom she was to be wed next day had tragically died. That very night she donned on her wedding dress and swore that she would never be parted from her love ever again. She ran out to the cliffs paying no heed to the thick fog that encircled her and jumped off the edge."

"That's all very well Arthur. But what's with the curse? If she committed suicide because her fiancé died, why did the family curse the house?" I pondered in bewilderment, shocked at my gullibility at believing the story so readily.

"Hmm. Good question that." Arthur answered scratching his head, "Well it's just a legend. There's no proof any of that happened. Only, you saw a photo and we've both seen the hair in the box. Does the hair match the girl would you say?"

"Definitely," I replied, bobbing my head up and down, "Michael has her photo, I took a picture on my phone."

Arthur leaned over my arm to take a look at the picture, "Wasn't she a beauty? What if there is some truth in the story and this is proof Amy was an actual being?"

"We need to find out more. See if the rest of the story is true and find out more about this supposed curse."

*

The next morning bells were pealing in the distance calling the locals to Church. I was surprised it was Sunday again, it had been more than a week since my arrival in Morecombe. Linda was calling me from downstairs letting me know that I had barely ten minutes to get ready if I wanted to be at Church on time. Arthur was reversing the car out of the drive as I opened the front door, struggling to get my arm into my turned-out coat sleeve.

It was a very long sermon on chapter 21 of Proverbs based on how to live righteously and doing what is right in the eyes of God and not in the ways of wicked men.

"When justice is done!" Nigel cried out, raising his arms up to the ceiling, "It brings joy to the righteous but terror to evildoers."

"Amen!" answered the worshippers.

I noticed that Ann held a tissue to her eyes, noticing me watching she gave a small smile. The service closed with a dirge 'How Great Thou Art,' every time I thought the song had ended another verse was sung. Bored and unfamiliar with the song, not being a

Church goer myself, I found myself glancing around the room. I recognised a few of the locals now, the lady from the post office, Mark and his family. Cathy, Sylvia and Ann were together, the Storms obviously, Brian from the pub with his parents. The Hopes were sitting near to the front, Roger must have sensed me staring for he turned and gave a small nod. I didn't see Lydia or Michael, I wasn't surprised that Michael wasn't there he didn't strike me as a Church person, but why wasn't Lydia there? The Vicar said a few more words and a prayer before announcing the end of service blessing.

Arthur loosened his tie and muttered, "And that is that for another week!"

After talking to a few new people, I swiftly made my excuses and dawdled at the bottom of the path waiting for my ride back. Three elderly ladies were chatting excitedly and huddled together to hear each other better over the roaring wind. I waved as I was recognised and not appearing to be rude, I walked over.

"Morning Tom. How was the service? Wasn't it grand!" Cathy exclaimed with virtue in her voice. "Justice will be served, and we will rejoice!"

"If you say so." I stammered, for I didn't have a clue what the service was about and had nodded off halfway through.

"Lunch at the vicarage Detective Tom? Nigel does a great roast chicken, unfortunately he does burn the veg like and the potatoes do dry out." Ann politely asked, "Cathy and Sylvia will be joining us so I'm sure Nigel will be grateful like for another man at the table."

"I would love to, I'll let Linda know I don't need a lift back."

"See you there then."

It took a while to find Linda she was nowhere to be found. Arthur was in the refreshment lobby helping himself to more cake. I explained the situation and he replied with a nod and a pat on my back, unable to speak having underestimated the stickiness of the cake he had just placed in his mouth.

At the vicarage I found myself sitting in the same place, the ladies squashed themselves together on the sofa and Nigel dragged the rocking chair over from its corner. He popped open a new bottle of elderflower cordial and carefully poured it out into small wine glasses. Must be a Sunday ritual, I thought to myself as I accepted my glass. The discussion was mainly about Christmas and the upcoming events in the village, when would be a good time to start the nativity play rehearsals. I was of no use to them, so I sat back and listened to them persuade and argue with each other, bringing new ideas to the table at every minute. Sylvia knew a place to find more holly and ivy, Cathy wanted to sort out the Church Christmas tree whilst Ann did decorations, and Nigel was going to have a word with Michael about borrowing some animals. Ann shared a humorous story when Nigel borrowed a few sheep from a farm in St Louisham for the Nativity. They caused a riot in the church, pooped everywhere and as Jesus was being laid in the cradle, an aggressive ewe headbutted Nigel off the stage!

It was during lunch we found ourselves talking about the case, the ladies were wondering how much further I got. I enlightened them as best as I could, constantly going back on myself as I remembered more details I had forgotten.

"So where does that leave us?" Nigel asked and counted his fingers, "Colin Marsh, Grace and Nathan Barnes, and Tony the builder."

"Four suspects. Hmm." Cathy hummed and nodded her head, "They all sound suspicious, I agree with you on that Tom. Grace covered in blood, Colin with his recently fired gun."

"Nathan Barnes desperately wanting Grace for his wife." Sylvia added.

"And Tony?"

"Tony Baker was owed a lot of money for his services. He didn't get paid after all the work he had done." I explained, placing my fork and knife together.

"Unbelievable behaviour on the Forrester's part. I would be fuming if that was me." Cathy responded moodily. "Why didn't he sue?"

"He was in love with Grace and her parents were killed only a short time after, he didn't have the heart to ask her."

"So romantic." Sylvia sighed, "He must have been quite the gentleman."

"Yes well. Sounds like motive to me." Cathy retorted.

There was a slight pause in the room as I tried to figure out what was bothering me, "I have two people who have motives but couldn't possibly have done it, and two people who could have done it, but they have no motives. I need someone who witnessed the murders or something suspicious at least, maybe they saw someone running away or saw someone going in with a shotgun."

"Mmm yes." Nigel hawed and leaned back, "Tony does have motive, but he was probably at Church at the time. He was an extremely religious man, never missed a service when I became vicar. He is the last person who would commit murder."

"And Grace, like, she was such a sweet thing who adored her parents and bent over backwards just to care for them. Even was considering like throwing away her career just to look after them. She would never commit murder either." Ann put in and cleared up the plates. "My father on the other hand, he was up there shooting rabbits the morning it happened. But where is the motive like?"

"I didn't know he was shooting on the morning it happened!" I exclaimed.

"Yes. Unfortunately, he was."

"And that leaves Nathan." Cathy added with a sigh, "He wanted Grace badly, but would he shoot her parents just to have her? Impossible. No one in their right mind would kill the parents of the person you're in love with. And he wasn't there at the time either, he turned up later at Roger's house."

"Did Roger tell you that?" I asked curiously, reflecting on what Lydia mentioned about her father, the words he uttered still engrained on my brain, 'did you see their bloody faces?'

"He did. Grace turned up first at the Hopes place, covered in blood and then Nathan turned up later at the same time as the constabulary."

"Did Roger tell you the shots were fired from the doorway?"

"No. He didn't tell me that much. He's a dark horse is Roger, knows much and says nothing."

Roger. Why did he lie about Nathan turning up after the murders? Or did Nathan turn up after as Roger said, but had a quick glimpse at Grace's parents beforehand? There was only a fifteen-minute window between Grace finding her parents and the police turning up. How did Nathan get to the house so quick? Was he there already? Or was it a coincidence he was in the area at exactly the right time? Did he see or hear anything or anyone?

"I think I need to talk to Nathan again," I announced, emerging from my bubble just as pudding was served.

"After pudding you can," Sylvia answered with a twinkle in her eye as she poured custard over my hot syrup sponge.

The sky outside grew darker, it was only when Nigel stood up to turn on a light, I realised how late it was. Black clouds grew closer together as the first pelt of rain hit the window, a second later the precipitation poured aggressively against the glass. I graciously accepted a lift from Nigel, relieved not to walk back and drown myself like a soggy rat. The road was almost flooded and almost impossible to see, soon we turned onto a familiar bend just before the farm track. Fortunately, the gate was already propped open with a large rock. Steadily Nigel ascended the steep muddy slope. Rivers of water flowed down, and the windscreen wipers beat vigorously against the torrent of rain. Suddenly I caught a glimpse of a dark figure by the roadside, my heart raced for surely there can't be anyone walking in this weather. Nigel slowed down and applied the handbrake whilst I gave a large sigh of relief, it was a live person out walking and must have got caught in the rain. Nigel loudly rapped on my window, recognising the figure next to him I hopped out of the vehicle and offered her my seat before jumping into the back.

"Hello Lydia. What brings you this way?" I inquired, shaking my wet hair from my face as I slammed the rear door shut.

"I'm visiting Linda and Arthur. Every Sunday we have a few drinks together and a good talk amongst friends." Lydia replied, struggling to get comfortable in her wet clothes. "Damn weather, the rain wasn't predicted until later. I thought I had plenty of time to get there before it rained."

"English weather at its best," Nigel laughed and parked up next to The Pines. "Right, looks like you two will need to dash the last part. I'll let them know you're here."

He gave three loud long blasts of the horn, presently the front door opened, and Arthur squinted out into the darkness not recognising the car in the downpour. Me and Lydia ran quickly towards him and the warm comforting light that radiated from inside.

"Hi Arthur! We're here. Nigel was ever so good and gave me a lift the last part of the way," Lydia exclaimed and kissed him on the cheek.

Linda gasped in shock at the state of us in soaked clothing and immediately went out of her way to run first Lydia and then myself a hot bath. Lydia graciously accepted some dry clothes from Linda followed by a hot cup of tea.

"The potatoes are still cooking in the oven. I wasn't too sure when you or Lydia would arrive you see, knowing the Ferns though they probably made sure you ate plenty." Linda stated, placing a can of tuna under the electric can opener.

"I thought supper was at 7pm?" I grinned and ate a few pieces of sweetcorn that were leftover in the bowl.

Linda grinned back, "You're getting to know my schedule, Tom. Here's a bowl and the grated cheese is in the fridge. You can put it on the table when you're done. So how did it go with the vicar and his wife and her cronies?"

By the time I had finished describing my afternoon the dinner alarm went off, my stomach was already rumbling in earnest need for some food. Jacket potatoes were officially one of my favourite foods and I smothered mine with plenty of toppings. Arthur popped open a bottle of Chateau LaFleur and gave me a large wink as he poured out the red liquid into glasses. Linda sniffed her glass and took a small sip which she swished around her mouth.

"Mmm. Not bad, the local shop has delivered well." She murmured and took another swig.

I grinned at Arthur for I had assumed right. Linda couldn't tell the difference between a cheap wine and a vintage wine.

Arthur looked thoroughly upset, "Linda you should know. This is a vintage wine called Chateau LaFleur from I think 1897. Not some cheap wine from the local!"

"Arthur found it in the cellar of The Larches." I explained, also taking a large swig enjoying the aromatic flavours.

"Whatever were you doing in there?" Linda asked astonished, "Especially you Arthur, you're the last person on this earth who would crawl through a dirty and dusty place full of cobwebs."

"I was looking for the box that Lydia mentioned." I answered.

"Box? What box? You didn't say anything about a box? Is that why you were up there the other day? You were looking for it and only just found it with the help of my Arthur? Well, I always did say he has his uses when he finally does decide to pull a leg! And he has even brought back some very old and ripe wine which is an added bonus in my book!"

"So, what was in it?" Lydia asked from the other end of the table where she had been quietly sitting and listening.

"Not much, just some hair and a weird poem." I replied, "I assume the photo came from there. And I'm guessing the bracelet could have too."

"Bracelet? What bracelet?"

"I found a bracelet when I first went over there. Sean bought it for Jenny until I eventually found out it originally belonged to Michael's ex-wife. But after talking to Sean again, I realised it could have actually belonged to your mother."

"Do you still have it?" Lydia asked.

"Yes. It's upstairs." I answered. I politely made my excuses and dashed upstairs for a brief minute before returning to the table, "Here it is."

Lydia took the gold bracelet deftly from my hand and handled it with care, turning it around in her hand with her thumb, "Yes. It did belong to my mother. Well sort of. It belonged to my dad really, he kept it in a jewellery box on the windowsill and tried to persuade my mother to wear it every time they went somewhere fancy. She never did, she hated it. She pleaded with my father to get rid of it."

"Now you've established where the bracelet originally came from. What was in the poem?" Linda inquired, changing the subject as she scrapped up the last piece of her potato, "Was it something romantic? A love poem from him to her, reaching out in writing to his forbidden love. Or was it darker, a threatening poem from someone with a vengeance saying, I'll have your guts for garters! Or was it a secret message that only a spy would understand?"

"Yes, alright Linda!" Arthur interrupted, shaking his head at her vivid imagination, "It was actually a poem that was written by someone wanting revenge for the death of their daughter and signed off with a curse."

"How dreadful," Lydia tutted, "Who was the daughter?"

"We think it was the girl in the photo. I reckon it was her personal effects in the chest. Just need to find out who wrote the poem and why." I responded.

"Have you heard of the local story of the girl called Amy," Arthur asked, looking around the table intriguingly, "She took her own life when her lover died at sea."

"I have heard of something like it. I was under the impression she took her own life because her lover left her." Lydia replied and quickly explained, "When I was younger, I played truant from school and used to spend most of my time listening to the tales of sailors. I first heard the story from Cathy's husband just after he got back from a voyage."

"I didn't know Cathy was married?" I said, piling up the empty dinner plates.

"Well, they don't live together anymore, the marriage went sour right from the beginning. His name is John, John Finch. You'll find him by the quayside if you're lucky. He spends most of his time out on the sea and travelling along the south coast."

John Finch? I thought to myself. Amazing how these people just kept popping up in such a small village.

Would he be able to enlighten me with more details on the haunting of The Larches?

Chapter 16

The rain continued to pelt down through the night, Lydia ended up staying in the guest room having no desire to venture out into the storm. I could feel the windows rattling and the walls shaking against the ferocious wind, ok the walls weren't really shaking it was all my imagination. Yet still, I pulled my duvet up to my shoulders and glanced fearfully out of the window unable to sleep. I ended up reading a book until it was almost two in the morning, I turned off my light and sat by the window. Would the prowler turn up again? The weather was easing off now and the downpour had turned into a light comforting drizzle. Two fifteen came and went. I felt myself stiffen as two thirty approached and kept my eyes focused on the gate.

I awoke the next morning perched on the edge of the chair and with an uncomfortable crick in my neck. I realised I must have fallen asleep where I sat. Disappointed with myself I headed down to breakfast, everyone was up and tucking in heartily. Everyone had slept well despite the storm. Linda found a good storm rather comforting and helped her to sleep better. No-one had heard anything or saw anything. After breakfast Linda and Lydia had a café to open and Arthur had some cars to get ready for viewing and they soon left. It was too early in the morning for me, so I offered to tidy up and promised to lock up after myself. I wondered to myself what time fishermen would be up, rather early I reckoned to get their first catch of the day. It was nearly ten now, it was probably too late to head down to the quay, but it was worth a try!

I reached the quayside and wasn't surprised to see there was no-one about, the boats were pulled up high to the sea wall and attached with heavy chains. The weather was still murky and damp, the wind blew wild and kept tugging my hood off. I wandered around a bit admiring the large fishing boats and finally saw a man in bright yellow mac and trousers with a bright yellow waterproof hat. He was busy tinkering with the molluscs that clung tightly to the hull underside of his boat.

"Excuse me," I calmly spoke as the man looked up crossly as he heard me approach on the shingle, "I'm looking for someone. John Finch?"

"Aye. John?" The man responded and carried on with his work, "He'll be in his shack."

"Right. Where is his shack?"

"Over yonder." The fisherman pointed towards the bottom of the cliff, "Behind 'em rocks."

"Thank you."

I headed back in the direction I came from but along the seashore this time, making sure I kept close to the sea wall as possible as the tide ebbed its way in. Three rather dilapidated wooden houses stood neatly together right against the wall and were sheltered from the harshest of winds behind the large rocks that towered in front. An elderly man sat outside with a very brown and weathered face under his yellow hat and a shocking white beard against the tan. He was wearing bright yellow oilskins whilst holding a net and toying with some cord as he threaded it through and around the mesh. I was fascinated and watched for a while.

"Nothing to see here boy." He grunted and looked at me for a brief second before carrying on with his work.

"I'm looking for John?" I inquired.

"You found him."

"Great. I'm investigating The Larches and I was wondering…"

"Look son. I know everything that goes on around here. There's nothing that don't get past me. Whatever it is just spit it out and keep it real simple." John retaliated standing up and headed into his cabin.

"The local story about the girl Amy. What can you tell me about her?" I asked, following him inside.

"Now that's more like it," John stated in a raspy voice. He had placed a kettle on top of his little gas stove and spooned coffee granules into two metal mugs. He unfolded two wooden chairs that were leaning against a small table and invited me to sit down. "Amy. What have you been told so far?"

I retold the story Arthur had told me and included the cursed poem and Amy's possessions which I found in the house. "The only thing wrong with Arthur's story is that there is no curse involved, I was hoping you could help me?"

"That's because that man, he got it all wrong," John sneered and coughed gently, "You shouldn't listen to idle chitter chatter. Now as for me, I'm a descendant of Sam."

"Sam?"

"Yes Sam. He was the lover of Amy, but he didn't die at sea."

"He didn't?"

The kettle whistled shrilly, and steam filled the room, John sorted out the hot drinks and added biscuits to the little table, "No he didn't."

John was irritably echoing my sentences, so I decided to be clearer, "Tell me the whole story."

"Well," John began and dunked a hobnob into his coffee, "It was twilight. Sam and his father went out for their last catch of the day unaware of the fog that was creeping slowly into the bay. Unbeknownst to them another boat was waiting and lurking and using the fog to their advantage they captured Sam and his father and kept them hostage in the bottom of their boat. Sam's boat was left abandoned and smashed to smithereens on the rocks."

I must have gasped at this point for John looked at me knowingly and nodded.

"Yes," John continued, "You didn't know that did you? But there's more. You already know the ending of the story. Amy was so upset by the death of her fiancé whom she was to be wed next day that she threw herself onto the rocks. But this is what you didn't know."

"And what was it that I didn't know?" I asked pretending to be dumb.

"This is another story I tell you. Amy, now she was a very rich wealthy young lady. Morecombe Farm was an equestrian centre back then and they bred racing horses. Made a pretty penny from it too. Only the finest horse jockeys and groomers of that time were allowed to live in the cottages for convenience sake you see. And they lived there with their families. Amy fell in love with Sam, and they met often and then one day she told her family she was going to get married to Sam. Now her family didn't want that. So do you know what they did?"

"No. What did they do?"

"They kidnapped Sam and his father that foggy evening. Told her that he had died at sea and his boat was found dashed upon the rocks! She was so distraught she killed herself that very night, her family found her the next day. Sam and his father were eventually released but by then it was too late. Sam swore vengeance and placed Amy's things and a curse into her family's cottage hoping that the family would spend the rest of their days suffering. To this day I never believed in that curse until you brought it up. Amy's family moved away shortly after, and a new family moved in. But do you know what the strange thing is? Every family that has lived there has always had such terrible misfortune."

There was a pause as I recollected my thoughts, "So Arthur was nearly right with the tale. Apart from the fact that the boy didn't die at sea, and it was him and not the family who left the cursed box in the house."

John gave a disgruntled snort, "The story is better when it comes from the source. Pass me that baccy over there."

I stood up to grab the tobacco and passed it to John as another question came into my mind, "How long have you lived here John?"

"You're really asking me. What do I know about the deaths of Elsie and John Forrester?" He muttered lighting his pipe, "Nothing. I lived further down the coast at the time, only when me and Cathy married did I live here. That were a good few years after the murders."

"I'm sorry to hear about you and Cathy." I murmured quietly, hoping that I hadn't touched a nerve.

John chuckled, "Sorry!? I'm not sorry, best thing for us really. Now I got my nets to mend. Any other questions?"

I shook my head as I couldn't think of anything else to add. John stood up, "Well. It's been nice talking with you. Hope you enjoy your day."

We shook hands and parted, John showed me a convenient little footpath near to the shacks which lead to the road and made the walk so much easier than trudging back through wet sand. I just had one more couple to visit before heading over to St Louisham once more, the sun was attempting to make an appearance as it dodged in and out of the clouds. Approaching the unmistakable house, I noticed two new little red dragons had been added to the collection and were proudly sitting on the gateposts. I knocked firmly on the door.

"Hello. You're back. Come in, come in." Ian beckoned and waved me in.

"Hello Ian, good to see you again." I replied and walked through into the living room, "Hello again Lou, I hope you don't mind me dropping in like this?"

"Not at all." Lou beamed and patted the space on the sofa next to her. "Are you here with more questions?"

"Naturally." I responded, sitting down.

"Alice! We have a visitor! Bring out the best cake!" Ian called out towards the direction of the kitchen. "Now, what questions have you got for us Tom?"

"I found out the name of Grace's builder. He was called Tony."

"Ahh yes! Tony Baker. I remember him now, he died not too long ago."

"That's right. He was nearly ninety."

"What an age. Saying that, we're almost ninety now." Lou sighed, "Still, we've done well with our lives. I remember Tony well from those days, dashing handsome man and his body was so toned! Gracie would blush crimson every time she saw him."

"Apparently he had a crush on her too." I responded and felt my own self blush crimson, Alice had just walked in with a tray of sandwiches and cake, followed by a pot of tea and teacups.

"Thank you, Alice," Lou smiled and poured me a cup, "You know, I never knew Tony fancied Gracie. Do you think those two were secretly in love with each other? Because that would cause quite a scandal if they were having an affair! First there was Colin who was married and now Tony!"

I laughed and accepted an egg and cress sandwich, "I don't think they were having an affair. Tony was very devoted to his wife. Although he didn't ask Grace to pay up the money, even after her parents had died."

"Money? What money?" Ian asked confused.

"The Forrester's owed Tony fifteen grand in today's money for his services and refused to pay him when he left the job halfway through."

"Despicable, but so like John." Lou muttered and shook her head slowly to show her annoyance.

"What was John like?"

"He was a mean old fart," Ian retorted huffily, sitting up in his chair to receive his tea, "He was always shouting at people, telling people what he thought of them and never had a kind word to say about anyone."

"He was very hard to please," Lou put in, "And boy, did he hate Nathan! Whenever he went over to the house John would scream from the window at him to go away."

"Why did he hate Nathan so much?" I questioned.

"Well Nathan…how do I put this. You've met him…right? He's just arrogant and mean, controlling and he's just not a very nice person. John probably saw straight through him and saw him for who he is."

"Nathan is an arse, just like John was an arse." Ian muttered, revolving back on his favourite word to describe people he didn't like.

Before he could say anything else, Lou interrupted him, "Elsie however, she was such a peaceful and beautiful person. I remember when she and Gracie did small odd jobs, just to raise the money for the builders in the first place. She was in shock when John refused to pay, Gracie said she became ill and suffered a stroke just two days later."

"Will you be seeing him again?" Ian inquired.

"Who? Nathan? Yes, I'm heading that way later today."

"Well best get a move on, those clouds look menacing to me."

"We have a meet up later today," Lou explained, "If I knew you were coming…"

"No, it's ok. Thank you for your time." I raised myself from the sofa and made my way to the hallway and dressed myself for the weather, then called out goodbye. Alice held the door open for me and pressed a piece of paper into my hand. It was only when she closed the door in my face, I looked at the scrap she gave me and broadly grinned, finally I had her number.

*

Those menacing clouds from earlier had completely vanished by the time I arrived at the retirement home. With the sun now out and beaming down its radiating heat, I began to perspire and removed my winter clothing before heading inside. Remembering how hot it was inside from last time, I also removed my jumper and walked indoors in just a buttoned shirt. The receptionist was still there and hiding behind a different bunch of flowers this time, some tall yellow gladioli and gypsophila with various leaves in between. She looked up at me with some confusion as I strolled towards her casually dressed for summer.

"Afternoon sir. Can I help?" She asked still staring at me up and down.

"Yes. Can I talk to Nathan Barnes please?" I replied staring back.

The receptionist gave a small cough, "He will only accept appointments made by telephone. I'm sorry, you should have phoned first. Goodbye."

She briskly turned back to her computer and typed furiously away, completely ignoring me and the next man who had just walked in. Left with no choice I left. Spotting an open room to the left of me with an open opportunity I broadly grinned and walked in. I picked up the telephone and rang the retirement home number which was conveniently stuck on the phone base. After a few rings the receptionist picked up,

"Hello, St Louisham Retirement Home."

"Hello, I like to book an appointment with Nathan Barnes." I responded cheerily.

"Gosh, he is popular today." She exclaimed, "I have space at 2.30pm, will that suit you?"

"Perfectly." I replied, the lady asked a few more questions before replacing the receiver. I laughed to myself and sat down with a newspaper and waited. The hour passed by fairly quickly and I walked up to the receptionist once more,

"Nathan Barnes? I have an appointment at 2.30pm."

The woman went bright red, and her eyes flared, "Of all the cheek! Just go already. You know where you're going."

Feeling rather pleased with myself I headed upstairs to Nathan's room and knocked on his door. A rather feeble noise came through the thick wood which sounded like he was saying, come in.

"Hello Nathan. I was hoping we could talk again." I put out my hand and not getting a response quickly put my hand back in my pocket again before sitting down opposite him.

"Who are you?" The elderly chap asked and glared at me with tired eyes.

"Tom Jones. I visited you before. About a week ago now."

"No. I don't know you. What do you want?"

"Just to ask some questions. About Grace and the homicides at The Larches."

"The Larches? That was Grace's home, wasn't it?"

"Yes, and it was her parents who died."

"I don't remember." Nathan murmured and closed his eyes, "I can't help."

"Well, can you tell me something about Grace." I persisted, refusing to take no for an answer. "You married her a few weeks after the deaths happened, before Grace's parents were even buried. Why the rush?"

"I don't know. Grace wanted to get married, and I guess I was her knight in shining armour," Nathan slowly answered, his breath growing raspier, "I wanted to take her away from all that, marriage was the only option."

"Were you there when Grace's parents died? Some people think you arrived later, but your own words said otherwise. Your daughter Lydia, she heard you say, 'did you see their bloody faces,' which means you must have been there."

"Look Tom. It's Tom, isn't it? I'm a tired old man who has had enough of life. I can't answer any of your questions."

He closed his eyes and drew his blanket up to his chin, a gentle snoring noise erupted from his throat. I sat a while watching him, wondering to myself what kind of man he must have been when he was younger. Was there a chance that he could have told someone his secrets? I was getting nowhere with Nathan, so I rose out of my chair and headed to the door, it was just as I was about to turn the handle that Nathan suddenly spoke.

"It was 1958. Wasn't it? The deaths. Yes, I was there, and I saw them. There was nothing left of their faces."

I paused in shock and turned around to face him, "You saw them? Did you see anyone else?"

"Yes. Roger."

Chapter 17
1958

A man watched Grace leave from the field of corn in which he was hiding, he chewed noiselessly on a stalk of barley corn. Unable to shake off that feeling the house gave him, he knew that he had to go inside and face it. The back door was carelessly left unlocked, and he opened the door and let himself in, peering into the rooms to find what he came for. It was while he was standing in the living room that the mist came, he could feel her hair wrap around him and the smell of roses drug his senses. She had appeared once more to him. The man couldn't help but feel she had a message to deliver. He was willing to do anything for the woman he loved and held her hand as she guided him towards the gun cupboard. It was carelessly unlocked and left widely ajar. He reached forward and loaded the gun. Staring into her eyes he finally understood what he had to do, what must be done so they could live together once more in their home. It was their home by rights, the people living there now were intruding and had no right to live there. Quietly he followed her upstairs unaware of what was around him or where he was going. She pushed the bedroom door open with a loud creak and pointed to the bed. The loud noise startled the sleeping woman, and she awoke with a start,

"What are you doing here?" She asked and shook her husband who lay next to her. "John. Wake up! Please John."

"What?" John grumbled and opened an eye, "What is it woman? Can't you see I'm sleeping?"

"John. We have trouble. Look." Elsie stammered. Her eyes enlarged with fear as her face turned white.

John pushed himself into an upright position and saw the man standing by the doorway, "You! I told you to stay away! I never want to see you again! Didn't you listen to my warning!?"

The man ignored him and aimed the gun towards John's face closing his one bad eye and took fire. Elsie screamed and wailed, pleading for her life as she held onto her dead husband. The murderer took no notice and aimed the gun once more in her direction and fired the second round. He stared a while at the two dead bodies soaked in their own blood. He showed no emotion or understanding of what just happened. Yet everything was ok for the girl in the mist was smiling at him and took his hand once more and wrapped herself around his body.

"Nathan?" called a voice from somewhere in the darkness. "Nathan!"

Nathan placed his head into his hands and crouched down into the corner of the doorway trying to shake away the noise that pounded in his head. Someone reached down and pulled him up, he stumbled and staggered unable to use his legs whilst his arms were constantly being pulled backwards by the girl's hands. A bright light shone into his face and blinded him, this must be the end, his time must be up as heaven called down to him. A sharp pain hit the right side of his face followed by a cold electric shock which covered his body.

"What?" Nathan spluttered as water dripped off his chin and he jumped up from where he was laying, "Where am I?"

Roger was too numb for words unsure how to explain what he had just witnessed, he could only mutter, "What did you do Nathan?"

Nathan burst out into tears as he suddenly realised his recent nightmare was in fact actual reality, "I don't know Roger, she made me. It was the only way to give her back what was rightfully hers."

"Who are we talking about? Grace?" Roger asked in confusion, "What is rightfully hers? I don't understand."

"No not Grace. The girl that lives there, it's her house and she wanted it back. I would do anything for her." Nathan replied, restraining his tears.

"For goodness sake Nathan!" Roger hissed and shook Nathan by the shoulders, "You have just committed murder. You have to tell the police."

"NO!" Nathan shouted and pushed Roger away, "I can't. And you won't tell anyone either. Promise me Roger. I'm telling you. It wasn't me. It was all her!"

Roger groaned struggling on saying the right thing, "I can't tell the police that you murdered a couple because a girl ghost told you too. Still, it was you who killed them. Promise me you'll turn yourself in. Promise!"

Nathan numbly nodded, "Ok I will, but let me first tell Grace."

"She'll be home soon. Come on over to my place, we need a whiskey to steady our nerves."

*

Grace was surprised to find the back door to her home was wide open, she was so sure she had locked it.

Knowing that Nathan, he must have picked the lock on the front door again and let himself in.

"Nathan?" She called out and wandered around downstairs. There was no answer, either he had left, or she had carelessly forgotten to lock the back door. She pulled out some pans and began to peel the potatoes and prepare the rabbits and veg for lunch. After setting up a tray with tea and biscuits she carefully made her way upstairs to her parents' room.

"Mama. Are you awake? They all missed you at Church, kept asking how you were."

The scream Grace gave turned into a cry of fear and a wail of distraught, the tea tray she was carrying shattered on the floor smashing all the china that was balanced on it. She stood paralysed for a minute before flinging herself onto her dead parents, hugging them close to her chest, their bodies still slightly warm to the touch. There was nothing she could do but cry for her loss, all hopes of her parents dying peacefully in their beds were snatched away in the most brutal manner. A further ten minutes later she realised she had to tell someone, unfortunately Susan was away on Sundays, the only person besides her parents she could truly trust. Grace held her mother's hand promising to be back soon and made her way to the front door.

"Nathan!" Grace exclaimed, seeing him standing in the doorway blocking her from exiting. She wiped her red face, "I need to go to Roger and Diana's house, it's urgent. Can you move away from the doorway please?"

"Why are you covered in blood Grace?" Nathan casually asked, unshocked to see her in such a state and with her face red and blotchy.

"You wouldn't understand." She began shakily. Nathan ignored her and pushed his way past her and headed upstairs. He soon returned and demanded, "What did you do Grace?"

"What? I didn't do anything!" She wailed, "I swear it. I came home from Church and…Who would do this?"

Nathan walked over to the gun cupboard, "There's a gun missing. It doesn't look good for you Grace."

"Nathan. Why won't you believe me?"

Nathan gave her an evil smile of pure malice and took a step closer to her and grabbed her by the waist, "Marry me, Grace."

"What?" Grace stuttered attempting to get out of his firm grip. "No! I don't want to marry you!"

"Ok, but I'll tell the police you killed your parents. You are covered in blood and a gun is missing from your cupboard. I'll tell the police and everyone you know. You know how villagers are once gossip gets around and you'll be shamed as a murderer for the rest of your life guilty or not guilty."

Grace fell to the floor weeping unconsolably for her lost future, telling herself it would have been better if she was also killed along with her parents. Seeing no way out she silently nodded, "Ok."

Chapter 18
Present Day

Nathan had closed his eyes again and snorted quietly through a blocked nose. A nurse walked in with his medicine and afternoon tea, she awoke him and made sure that his pills went down his throat. She offered me a cup before heading out to the room next door.

Nathan looked at me and gave a weary smile, "1958. That was an unforgettable year of my life. I'm about to die any day now they tell me. I haven't got much longer to live. I haven't told anyone my story, not my wife or my children or grandchildren. You'll be the first. And you can tell who you want or keep it to yourself."

I leaned back in the chair and placed one leg on top of the other as a usual habit when listening to a long tale. It took a while for Nathan to get going and every so often he stopped to cough or take a swig of water. I listened spellbound in shock and then in mortified horror as Nathan reached the end of his tale, he finally concluded the story with,

"Now you know."

I was too stunned to say anything for a few minutes, the elderly man took the opportunity to shut his eyes once more and rest his heart which had accelerated as he retold his life.

"Why did you do it?" I asked, scratching my head.

"The girl. She told me too. I wanted to get the house back for her, for us, and it was the only way."

"Amy?"

"Is that her name?" Nathan looked alive for a second, "Well I hope she is waiting for me on the other side. She was so beautiful, so full of life and love."

For a moment I could have sworn the room filled with the scent of roses and the salty sea air, I could picture Amy so clear in my head she could have been standing next to me. Nathan must have been visualising her too for he put out his hand as if to grab hold of something.

"Amy," Nathan murmured, "Grace was the spit image of her. Did you know? That's why I was so desperate to hold onto Grace, she was my only connection to Amy. I used to fantasise she was Amy at times, but there were times when Grace came through and it made me so angry."

"What did you do with the shotgun?" I quietly asked.

"Threw it into the sea." Nathan silently replied. "Now I need my sleep. I just want to remember the past before I forget again."

"Sure Nathan. Just one more question. Tony Baker. Grace's family owed him a lot of money. Apparently, he visited you a couple of years later and you had an argument, Tony's son Mark remembers you arguing."

"Tony Baker. He was the builder, wasn't he? Yes, I remember. He wanted his money, and he was happy to settle for half of it. I can't remember how much but it was a lot. I put my foot down and said no, if John refused to pay then so would I."

Satisfied I stood up and took my cue, Nathan gave me a sad and weary look as I headed out of the door. The last thing I heard him say was,

"May God be my true witness of my crime."

I stood outside in the open and basked in the sunshine, I placed my head into my hands and groaned. A few elderly people sitting under the veranda stared at me and one even asked me what was wrong. Where do I start? Do I tell anyone or not? There was one person who knew, one person who could confirm the truth.

*

Roger's study was chilly, and clouds of steam rose from the hot cup of tea that I held. I had just retold Nathan's story to Roger, and I was now waiting for a response from the man. Roger just sat there, sighing every so often as he thought to himself on how best to approach this situation. Diana came in with some sandwiches and salad for us to share and sensing the awkward silence between me and Roger, swiftly left the room shutting the door firmly behind her.

"Well," Roger began. "You know everything now, I guess. What more can I tell you?"

"So, are you confirming that the confession is true?" I uncomfortably asked.

"It's all true. Every bit."

"So why didn't you tell me in the first place? Why beat around the bush?"

"I promised Nathan all those years ago that I would never tell a living soul, it was down to him you see to tell the police everything."

"But he didn't though. Did he?"

"Not quite no. He lied to me that day and I felt rather let down. I've never broken a promise in my life, and it was uncomfortable knowing what I knew." Roger leaned forward and took a cheese and cucumber sandwich, "It didn't help either that Nathan refused to help the police with their investigation. And every time the police officers tried to convict Grace he was always there to say, 'no it wasn't her'."

"Did you know that Nathan forced Grace's hand in marriage?" I mumbled as I munched on some crunchy lettuce.

"No. He didn't tell me that. That was a shock when you told me. Makes sense now why Grace married him, I never did understand her actions at the time. She completely loathed the man."

"Is it possible to hear your version of events? Nathan told me he killed Mr and Mrs Forrester because the girl Amy told him to."

"Who's Amy?"

"She used to live at The Larches and died on the cliffs right by the house. She continues to live there. Nathan said he killed Grace's parents because him and Amy wanted their house back."

Roger sat back in his armchair and pulled out a cigar, "That explains his mood then. I'll tell you my version and see if it adds up. It was earlier that day can't remember the time. It was early morning sometime before Church. Diana was pruning some roses when Colin Marsh went shuffling past in the direction of home, his whole arm completely covered in blood. I had heard shots from earlier and so I assumed he had a hunting accident when taking pot-shots at some game. Then Grace went by about half an hour later, she had obviously been crying her eyes out at some point. Diana called out to her to see if she was ok. Boys causing trouble is what Grace had said between Colin and Nathan."

Roger paused to take a swig of coffee and light his cigar and continued,

"Anyway, it was sometime later that I realised I hadn't seen Nathan, usually I hear his dreadful whistle when he walks past. Diana hadn't seen him go past the house either. He wouldn't be at the farm because it was Susan and Jeff's day off. So, I decided I'd better head over to The Larches to see if everything was ok, it wasn't. Now this will sound strange to you. I looked in through the front window and I saw Nathan unlock the cupboard in the dining room and pull out a shotgun. Fearing the worst, I shook the front door and rattled the windows trying to get in. And Nathan, he was completely oblivious. He was walking in some kind of trance unaware of what he was doing, he was like a zombie. He headed up the stairs and I could no longer see him, so I went round the back, fortunately the back door was wide open. I ran upstairs as fast as I could in time to see him kill Grace's parents from the doorway in which he stood. Nathan just stood there still in his trance. I don't think he had any idea of what he had just done. I dragged him outside and smacked his face and poured water over him and he soon came to."

"Do you think that Nathan was possessed?" I curiously asked, giving way to my scepticism.

"I don't believe in that nonsense. When you die that's it. You either go up or down depending. Yet, when I saw Nathan's face, I was truly scared, he didn't look like Nathan at all. It was as if someone else was controlling him and using his body." Said Roger quietly and then burst out laughing, "What a load of tosh! I must be getting old. Just ignore me it was a long time ago."

"And the house? Do you think it's haunted?"

"Definitely not. I've been there a few times, and nothing has ever happened to me. If you met John, he would also agree with me. Nothing wrong with that house at all!"

"So, you haven't seen anyone hanging around late at night?"

"Not lately no. Only the girl Jenny, but you know about that already."

I nodded. Yes, Jenny and Daniel. Two people who died right near The Larches in an accidental death, in the middle of the night in a dense fog. I had just one more question to ask of Roger,

"Why did you lose contact with Nathan? He told me you no longer speak to him." I questioned, placing my empty cup on the table.

"Well, I had to work with him at the farm, knowing that he was a murderer. That was hard and watching him bully Grace continuously and finding fault when there wasn't any to find. It was such a relief when he got dementia and finally had to slow down, I hardly saw him anymore after that."

"Thank you, Roger. Is there anything you haven't told me? I pretty much know everything now, but I want to make sure that nothing is left out this time."

Roger smiled, "No that's everything Tom. You've got Nathan's confession now and mine to back it up. What are you going to do about it?"

"I don't know yet Roger, I'll need to think about it. The crime wasn't written down, or it was written and got lost, I don't know. Either way, without a report it's impossible to convict someone of a crime that doesn't exist in the police files."

"Very true. But what about Nathan's family? The villagers? Will they be told?"

"I don't know. Nathan should pay for his crime and yet he's an old man about to die any day now. Should we wait till after his death? And Colin, he's been accused of the crime all these years, his name should surely be cleared."

"Yes. I'm sorry I tried to convince you it was Colin. Very unjust of me. Well, whatever the outcome, make sure I'm the first to know."

"Will do. I'll let Ann know her father wasn't guilty. And Linda will probably get a confession out of me before the day is over!"

Roger chuckled, "That Linda! Just make sure she doesn't spread gossip. We don't want any more rumours. Do we?"

I stood up and shook Roger's hand hoping this time Roger had been true to his word and confessed everything and wasn't holding back vital information.

Diana waved goodbye from the window, she looked very distracted in thought, must have been eavesdropping.

*

It was late afternoon by the time I rang the doorbell of the vicarage, Nigel was out on his errands visiting his local parishioners. Ann had just returned from a visit to the village, so I was fortunate to call round when I did. She could tell by the look on my face that I had some big news to tell her.

"Better make it a large gin and tonic then." She said and showed me through to the living room. Ann opened a small cupboard and poured out some drinks for us and explained, "Nigel doesn't appreciate drinking unless it's like serious."

I subduedly nodded my head, "It's serious Ann."

"Right." Was the only thing Ann could say so I told her the outcome of the investigation, "It wasn't Colin…Ann. It wasn't your father."

Ann wept and cried silent tears, "Thank you Tom. Like I always knew that it wasn't him. He was a wild character but not a murderer."

"It turns out you were right about the rabbits," I plundered on, "He was shooting up there on the day. Nathan can testify for him."

"Then why didn't Nathan say he saw him? Why didn't Nathan confess to the murders? Why let my father like take all the blame?"

"I don't know. Nathan hated Colin with a passion. Your father was madly in love with Grace and Nathan wasn't having any of that. He probably wanted your father to go to prison for a crime he didn't commit and instead had to live with your father presumed guilty and not convicted guilty."

"What happened to the gun that killed the Forrester's?

"Nathan threw it into the sea apparently."

Ann nodded and gulped down the rest of her drink which was still half full and bravely smiled, "That's better. I'm not surprised to hear Nathan was like the murderer. But I am surprised at Roger, holding onto such a dark secret. What made him like not tell anyone? After all these years?"

"Roger promised Nathan." I began and was immediately interrupted.

"Rubbish! You can break a promise when the law gets involved. Roger was probably scared he would be arrested for holding back vital information."

I nodded my head in agreement, "Well I'll leave you now, just thought you would like to hear the news."

Ann hugged me and whispered in my ear, "Thank you so much Tom. Like you have no idea how much this means to me."

I looked at Ann and saw how much younger in face she looked and how she walked more upright than ever. A key rattled in the front door and the door swung open, Nigel took one look at me and then Ann who was positively beaming.

I smiled at Nigel, "It's good news Nigel. Ann can tell you everything, I need to head back."

I closed the door behind me and whistled as I walked back towards the village, the wind blew savagely around me sending shivers down my body. I was too happy with a successful outcome to be bothered by such a trifle thing. The clouds drifted apart, and the moon shone down, bathing the village in a mystical white light. The sharp contrast of monotone colours gave me the feeling of walking through a black and white picture.

*

"There he is! The wanderer has returned home! Where have you been? It's gone 7pm, your supper is cold, and I'll need to reheat it. It won't taste the same mind you, better when it's fresh off the stove. Come in quickly Tom, there's a cold wind blowing. Lucky for Arthur that I didn't send him out to search for you, he would have been frozen to the core by now!"

"Hello Linda!" I broadly smiled and kissed her on the cheek and called through to the living room, "Evening Arthur!"

"Well! Look at the cat who got all the cream! You've got great news. Oh, you've got to tell me!" Linda clapped her hands in excitement, "Wait! Don't tell me just yet, let me get you a beer and reheat your supper."

Obediently I sat down next to Arthur who was transfixed on the television, the scores were close, and a goal was imminent. Linda walked through with my supper on a tray just as me and Arthur shouted, "Goal!"

Linda stood in front of the television and firmly turned it off, "You can watch that later Arthur, Tom has some exciting news to share."

For the third time that day I told the rest of the story, watching the faces of Linda and Arthur turn bright red with excitement and their eyes grow wider.

"So, it was Nathan?" Linda exclaimed, "Well who'd have thought it? And to think we live next door to his accomplice!"

"Roger's not an accomplice Linda, he's a key witness." Arthur explained and tutted.

"A key witness who didn't say anything. No, I reckon I'm right. Roger and Nathan must have been in it together, it's the only thing that makes sense. If you murdered someone Arthur I wouldn't tell a living soul, I would even help you to bury the body!"

"Now you're talking daft woman!" Arthur intervened. "Roger didn't kill anyone. We've just heard that Nathan confessed, and Roger backed up that confession. Nathan as you very well know is a liar and if he was in it with Roger, he would make sure that he would shift the blame from himself onto Roger!"

There was a pause as Linda muddled through the problematic situation, "Ok Arthur, you win. I still can't figure out why Roger didn't say anything after all this time."

"Ann reckons he didn't want to get involved with the police and get arrested for holding back important information." I answered as a soggy chip fell off my fork.

"You spoke to Ann? What did she have to say on the matter?" Arthur asked.

"I had to let her know that her father Colin wasn't the killer. Her opinion on the investigation is the same as yours. There is no doubt in my mind that it was Nathan and Nathan only." I concluded.

"Have you told anyone else?"

"No. I thought I'd keep it that way until Nathan dies, he hasn't got much longer to live."

"Where does that leave Roger? Does he get involved in the story?" Linda quietly inquired.

"No. It's best to leave him out." I silently replied hoping that my decision was the right one.

It was past midnight by the time Linda and Arthur made their excuses and headed up to bed, I couldn't sleep after such an exciting day. I tried to read a book with no success, so I ended up lying on my bed counting sheep. Suddenly I woke up startled and sat upright in my bed, I rubbed my eyes with my finger and thumb realising I must have fallen asleep at some point. But what had just made me wake up? I peered out of the curtains and saw nothing, only the moon which was desperately trying to break through a thick dense cloud. I glanced at my phone. It was almost quarter past two in the morning. Not taking any chances I hurriedly dressed and waited. I must have almost fallen asleep again for I was woken by a familiar noise. Quickly I looked through the window and to my astonishment the prowler was back and lurking by the swinging gate. I dashed downstairs and undid the latch on the back door and swung the door open, carelessly forgetting to close it in my haste. The person must have heard me for they swiftly got a move on and headed up the coastal path in the direction of Morecombe Farm. I raced through the gate and noticed the figure walking off at a slower rate now, silently I followed behind. There were times when I struggled to see properly, and the person kept disappearing from view. I patted my pockets urgently and realised I left my torch behind. The clouds were getting thicker and lower by the minute as a dense fog creeped in from the sea. Furious with myself, I cursed under my breath as my target completely vanished from view. I turned around a few times on the spot, hoping to catch a glimpse of the person and then suddenly I did. They were just standing there, a few feet in front with their back to me. I could make out long dark hair that almost reached the waist. I called out to whoever it was,

"Hello? Who are you? What are you doing up here?"

I didn't get a reply and as I stood there watching, I noticed that the fog didn't go around them or move in a particular fashion, it just hovered motionless. Desperate to get to them I stepped forwards and immediately regretted it, the figure turned and headed towards the sea. Fearing the worst, I quickly ran over to them,

"NO! Don't! Stop!"

All of a sudden, my left leg was no longer touching the ground, it dangled in mid-air and with the shock of having no land under me my whole left body fell sideways. Petrified out of my wits my hands lunged out and grabbed whatever it could find in the darkness as the rest of my body slid off the edge of the cliff. I could only feel wet grass, coarse roots and rough pebbles which slowly gave way; my feet beneath scrambled for a rock or a ledge in aid of support. With relief I managed to hold onto what felt like a large stone with the tips of my fingers. For a while I was reassured and somewhat calmer as my other hand reached for the stone. The ledge was extremely narrow, and my fingers burnt with pain, desperate to get back up to the top I kicked out with my legs hoping to find something to relief the pressure. This can't be happening, I told myself, as one by one my fingers slowly gave up the fight. I closed my eyes as I knew the end was imminent and closer than ever before.

"GOT YOU!"

I opened my eyes as an angel surrounded in a great beam of light grabbed hold of my wrist and began to pull me up. It was only when I got closer to my rescuer I realised.

"Arthur." I stammered numbly and promptly sat down on the damp grass as my body was still in complete shock.

"You're alright Tom. I got here just in time." Arthur replied and also sat down next to me, placing the searchlight between us, "That was my first ever rescue. How did I do?"

I wanted to laugh but I didn't know how too so I silently answered, "Just great. Thank you. How did you find me?"

"Well, the gate was open again. I went to shut it and realised the back door was open too. And then I saw you wandering off into the fog. I thought to myself, that can't be good. So, I followed you."

"Did you see the figure I was following?"

Arthur looked confused for a moment, "I didn't see anyone else. Lucky I followed you, eh? Although I did lose you in the fog for a few minutes. Why didn't you take a torch?"

"I forgot," were the only words I could manage to mumble from utter exhaustion.

"I think we should head back, Linda will be worried about us," Arthur helped raise me up onto shaky legs and I was thankful for someone to lean on and guide me home. The fog was clearing up now and the moon managed to peek out for just a brief minute. It was in that minute that I realised where I was. I found my head turning in the direction of The Larches, particularly the downstairs window. A girl with dark brown hair with sweet lips upon a kindly face, wearing a long white dress with laced sleeves gazed forlornly at me. I couldn't help but stare at her. The misty moon disappeared behind the clouds once more. And just like that, so had she.

About the Author

J.M.G.Smith grew up in the Chilterns and is where she got her inspiration and ideas for many of her characters. The ideas for picturesque scenery and panorama sea views came from her many travels to seaside villages surrounded by cliffs. Originally a keen gardener, she learnt horticulture at the Berkshire College of Agriculture before taking up the trade landscaping. J.M.G.Smith now lives in Nottingham with her husband and four children and has settled down to domestic duties, pot gardening at home and busily writing her next book.